THE RAPTOR OF THE HIGHLANDS

BOOK THREE OF THE SYLVAN CHRONICLES

PETER WACHT

Kestrel
Media Group, LLC

The Raptor of the Highlands

By Peter Wacht

Book Three of The Sylvan Chronicles

This book is a work of fiction. Names, characters, places, and incidents are the product of the author's imagination or are used fictitiously. Any resemblance to actual events, locales, or persons, living or dead, is coincidental.

Copyright 2019 © by Peter Wacht

Cover design by Ebooklaunch.com

All rights reserved. In accordance with the U.S. Copyright Act of 1976, the scanning, uploading, and electronic sharing of any part of this book without the permission of the publisher constitute unlawful piracy and theft of the author's intellectual property.

Published in the United States by Kestrel Media Group LLC.

ISBN: 978-1-950236-04-6

eBook ISBN: 978-1-950236-05-3

Library of Congress Control Number: 2019905673

❀ Created with Vellum

ALSO BY PETER WACHT

THE REALMS OF THE TALENT AND THE CURSE

THE TALES OF CALEDONIA

(Complete 7-Book Series)

Blood on the White Sand (short story)*

The Diamond Thief (short story)*

The Protector

The Protector's Quest

The Protector's Vengeance

The Protector's Sacrifice

The Protector's Reckoning

The Protector's Resolve

The Protector's Victory

TALES OF THE TERRITORIES

A Fate Worse Than Death (short story)*

Stalking the Red Ruby (short story)*

Death on the Burnt Ocean (Forthcoming 2023)

Monsters in the Mist (Forthcoming 2023)

The Dance of the Daggers (Forthcoming 2023)

THE SYLVAN CHRONICLES

(Complete 9-Book Series)

The Legend of the Kestrel

The Call of the Sylvana

The Raptor of the Highlands

The Makings of a Warrior

The Lord of the Highlands

The Lost Kestrel Found

The Claiming of the Highlands

The Fight Against the Dark

The Defender of the Light

THE RISE OF THE SYLVAN WARRIORS

Through the Knife's Edge (short story)*

* Free short stories can be downloaded from my author website at www.PeterWachtBooks.com.

*For my parents.
Thank you for me teaching me
that persistence and hard work,
and some stubbornness,
pay off.*

YOUR FREE SHORT STORY IS WAITING

THROUGH THE KNIFE'S EDGE

This short story is a prelude to the events in *The Sylvan Chronicles* and is free to readers who receive my newsletter.

Sign up and get your free copy at www.PeterWachtBooks.com.

1

______

A FRIEND

The dreams swept through his mind like a tidal wave. In the first, he stood on a huge promontory looking out over a drop of a thousand feet. The wind tugged at him, wanting to pull him to his death, but he resisted. Power coursed within him. He held the Sword of the Highlands above his head in triumph, and for the first time he felt free — and in control of his own destiny.

That dream disintegrated, replaced by another. He stood in the middle of a pit with soft, white sand beneath his feet. The walls of the pit, twenty feet high and made of a glassy stone, appeared impossible to climb. He gripped a spear in his hand, but it was like none he had ever seen before. It resembled a quarterstaff, but even that term wasn't quite right because of the long, sharp blades affixed to its ends. Blood covered his body; some of it his own, most of it not.

He couldn't remember what had happened, but again he experienced a momentary thrill of exultation. He had won. He had survived! This time, though, that feeling disappeared when his gaze traveled out of the pit to the stands situated around it, where lords and ladies watched him, looks of surprise and wonder on their faces. His eyes went from one arrogant or fearful expression to the next, until he stopped at one. The girl. The girl from the Burren. Kaylie. Instead of feeling happy at seeing her beautiful, blue eyes, though, he felt betrayed. Betrayed by her.

Another dream entered his mind, pushing the other one out. He knelt on a windswept slope, the gritty black dirt staining his breeks. It was daytime, but the dark, churning clouds created a perpetual dusk. Blackened mountains towered above him. The wind twisted and turned around the peaks, carrying fragments of sound. He concentrated as best he could, but found it difficult. He was tired. His energy almost gone. He had been searching for something, something that would allow him to escape the cold, the fear. But he had failed. The Key was now beyond his grasp.

Finally, after several frustrating minutes, the fragments of sound became words in his ears, the whispers teasing him, pushing at the bounds of his sanity. He tried to fight it, to hold back the madness seeping into his brain, but he could struggle for only so long. He fell forward in the black dirt, a dark haze covering his mind. The words finally made sense: *The shadow rules. The shadow rules. Death to those who oppose the shadow.* As the darkness swept him away, he knew that he would never wake again.

The dreams came faster and faster, speeding through his mind, making it impossible for him to remember them all. He knew they were important, that they affected his life in some way. If only he could decipher them and find out what messages they contained. But the dreams only increased in speed, swirling around in his head like a tornado. He wanted to escape, to flee from his own mind, but he didn't know how. Then the dreams disappeared, replaced by a bright light.

Thomas enjoyed the calm and quiet after enduring the whirlwind in his head. Slowly, the light grew stronger, forcing his eyes open. His head exploded in pain. He pushed himself up to a seated position, squinting because of the bright sunlight and rubbing the side of his head with his hand. At least he tried to. The shackles on his wrists prevented it. With some careful maneuvering, he was finally able to do it. A lump had formed there, just above the ear. Other than that, he was fine, except, of course, for the tremendous headache. Then he remembered everything.

He had tried to help that group of Highlanders the reivers had captured, and though he had succeeded in freeing them, he now faced the same predicament himself. His grandfather had been right. Eventually the risks would catch up to him, and in this particular instance they had. He hated when Rynlin was right! At least he wouldn't have to see the look of smugness his grandfather so enjoyed giving him. Actually, considering his present circumstances, that look of smugness probably wouldn't be so bad.

Opening his eyes fully, he winced. The early morning sun had not yet burned off the dew from the grass, which helped to explain why his shirt and breeks were damp. He turned his head from side to side, surveying his position. He was in the middle of the reivers' camp, or what was left of it anyway. Most of the reivers had formed into a long line of two horseman abreast, while a few struggled to pull down the tent.

"Good morning."

Thomas shifted around slowly, gasping for breath because of the sharp pain that shot through his head from the movement. The pounding in his head increased. The large boy stared back at him, his face a mass of welts and bruises, his long blond hair matted down by blood and dirt. He had tied a strip of cloth around the wound on his right arm. The boy looked to be his own age, though he was massive. Thomas felt like a dwarf sitting there across from him. His surrender had served a

purpose at least. The reivers hadn't killed the Highlander —
yet.

"How long have I been out?"

"Two hours," replied the boy.

Thomas grunted in reply. Two hours. It had felt like an eternity. And those dreams. They were important. He needed to
remember them. But he couldn't. Bits and pieces flirted with his
memory, but the puzzle refused to form.

"How's your arm?"

The large boy grunted. "As good as can be expected. Just a
scratch really."

"You should have escaped when you had the chance," said
Thomas, gingerly rubbing at his head. He had to do it carefully,
otherwise he might hit himself in the head with the chains
attached to the shackles, and his headache was bad enough
already.

"I know. But I couldn't let you have all the fun. It wouldn't
have been fair." The boy looked at the eight reivers stationed
around them with hate-filled eyes.

"Well, that explains everything," said Thomas.

The boy smiled. "Thank you for freeing my people. A debt
is owed. Whenever you have need, it will be repaid."

Thomas was going to tell him that it wasn't necessary, that
there was no need to repay the debt. The intensity in the boy's
eyes made him think better of it. He had been away from his
people for a long time and forgotten some of the customs. This
one came back to him quickly. If one Highlander made a
personal sacrifice for the benefit of another Highlander, such as
a Marcher saving another Marcher's life, the person would say,
"A debt is owed." Men of honor did not scoff at such a statement, as it was never said lightly.

"When I have need," replied Thomas, remembering the
correct response.

The boy nodded. "You look like a Highlander, but then again, you don't."

It was a strange thing to say, but Thomas understood. "I am a Highlander. My mother wasn't."

The large boy nodded again. He studied Thomas critically for a few moments. "You fight well, green eyes. My name is Kylin, but my friends call me Oso."

"A strong name, Oso. My name is Thomas."

"That, too, is a strong name. Well met, Thomas."

Oso tried to extend his hand in greeting, but the chains held him back.

"So, the two young heroes are awake," said Killeran, walking past the eight guards and standing over them. "Good. It is time to go to your new home, or rather what will serve as your home until you die."

Killeran thought that the last portion of his statement would register with the two. They were young, with long lives ahead of them, or rather they did before their capture. But they ignored him, giving him only steely glances. He couldn't tell which one wanted him dead the most -- the large one or the one with green eyes. Green eyes? Why did that tug at his memory? He tried to remember for a moment, then gave up.

"You have cost me twenty able-bodied workers, and more than a dozen reivers, so it looks like you will have to do the work of all. No matter. You'll simply die sooner."

Killeran studied his two new prisoners, still expecting a reaction. But there wasn't one. They were still proud, still confident. By the end of the day, though, he'd have them blubbering like children.

"Bring them," he said, motioning to the reivers.

The reivers half-dragged, half-carried Thomas and Oso to the end of the two cavalry columns, then affixed long chains to their collars. Two reivers at the end of the column grasped the leashes.

The reivers then placed chains around their ankles, with a two-foot length attached to their leg shackles. They would have a very hard time going faster than a slow walk, as neither could extend their legs more than a foot at a time. Of course, Killeran didn't plan for them to walk very far at all. These two boys intrigued him, and the one with green eyes moreso than the other. Why? Why should that bother him so? He shook his head in frustration.

Killeran wiped his sleeve across his nose. His cold hadn't gotten any better. If he had to suffer through another miserable day in this inhospitable land, then these two could do so in a slightly different way. Satisfied that his prisoners were prepared for the day's journey back into the foothills, Killeran walked up to the front of the column and climbed onto his horse. Cutting the air sharply with his arm, the column started forward.

They had traveled for no more than a few minutes before he heard a satisfying sound that made him smile. Turning in his saddle, he saw that the large boy had tripped over a rock and was having a hard time getting up again because of the chains. He was dragged a short distance before he finally regained his feet. It looked like it just might be a very good day. Later in the morning he would pick up the pace and let the horses stretch their legs. Yes, it would be a very good day indeed.

2

A DRAG

Thomas tasted dirt for the twentieth time that day. Spitting the grainy particles out of his mouth, he glanced at his companion sharing in the misery. Oso looked just as bad as Thomas felt. His body demanded that he stop and lay there for the next ten years. Every muscle burned, every bone ached. He ignored the pain and forced himself to rise as quickly as he could, not wanting to get dragged across the rocky soil again. The chains around his ankles weighed him down, impeding his efforts.

He stumbled for the first few yards as he struggled to maintain his balance and resume the awkward gait the chains required. The reiver holding on to the leash attached to his collar didn't care about Thomas' struggles. In fact, he rather enjoyed them, putting heel to horse whenever he fell to make things just a little more difficult. And this was the easy part, when the horses moved at a walk. Trying to keep pace with the column at a trot with a short length of chain attached to your ankles just didn't work. Once you fell down, you couldn't get back up. All you could do was try to avoid the larger rocks or stones that his guard had a particular knack for finding.

They had traveled since early morning, Killeran very intent upon getting somewhere fast and not allowing anything to slow him down. Several times during the day he had ridden to the back of the column to check on them. Each time afterward he quickened the column's pace, taking a special glee in the two boys' constant falls.

Thomas again looked over at Oso, who trudged along beside him. Oso's size was intimidating, but he was remarkably quick and agile for one so big. Nevertheless, he had spent a lot more time getting dragged behind his jailer's horse than Thomas had behind his, and it showed. Now the rest of his body matched his face, covered in welts and bruises and cuts. The wound on his arm had reopened. His clothes were torn in a dozen places and he was caked in mud and dirt. Thomas knew his condition was just as bad. On the bright side, though, his headache was gone. In fact, that was the only part of his body that didn't hurt at the moment.

He wondered what Rya would have done if he had come home looking like this. He smiled to himself thinking about it. She'd probably have a fit. Thomas pushed the thought from his mind. He didn't have time to think about that. He needed to find a way to escape, yet all he could do at the moment was concentrate on his feet. If his chains got tangled, he'd never get back up. At least it was getting dark. Soon they'd have to stop, then Thomas could concentrate on escaping.

3

———

IGNORED TAUNTS

Evening reluctantly gave way to night, and Thomas was thankful for the opportunity to rest. His entire body hurt. The reivers who served as their jailers had dragged Thomas and Oso into the middle of the camp where a lone tree stood in the center of the clearing. Suddenly, Thomas fell forward, landing hard on the ground. Thomas' jailer grinned after having kicked him in the small of his back. The other reiver produced a chain and wrapped it around the trunk of the tree, then affixed it to their chains as well.

Oso dropped to the ground next to Thomas, leaning against the tree. They were completely exhausted. Neither had a drop of energy left. It was several minutes before either could speak, and even then it was through gasps for breath.

"So, do I look as bad as I feel?" asked Oso, stretching his long legs out in front of him. His muscles screamed in protest, but he ignored them. He readjusted the strip of cloth and tightened it around his arm. That should stop the bleeding.

"Worse," replied Thomas. He wasn't as winded as Oso. He had Rynlin and Rya to thank for that. His constant training had helped him greatly during the day's ordeal.

Oso tried to laugh, and instead it came out as a wheeze, finding it difficult while catching his breath. He sounded like Tigan, an old man in his village who laughed so hard that sometimes his face turned a bright red from the lack of air.

"So how's your head?"

"It's the least of my worries right now," replied Thomas. "And your arm?"

"Like you, the least of my worries."

"Well, it was a pleasant day nonetheless," said Thomas, finding that talking helped to take his mind away from the bolts of pain that shot through his legs. He tried to stretch them out but had to stop halfway. They were cramping up, the sharp pain reawakening his senses. He'd try again in a few minutes. "A warm sun. A pleasant breeze. It's always nice to be outside on a day like this."

Oso looked over at his new friend as if something had been rattled in the smaller boy's head during one of his falls.

Thomas explained himself. "It helps to take away the ache when your mind focuses on something else."

Oso nodded, then tried it himself. He imagined that he was back near his village, stalking a large buck that had wondered close to his hiding place. In absolute silence, he affixed an arrow to his bow and stepped out from between two large trees. He stepped slowly through the brush, careful not to disturb anything that would give him away to his quarry. It was good to hunt again. To feel the rush of adrenaline as you closed in for the kill. He just needed to get a little closer. Just a little closer. He pulled back the bow, the string almost touching his face. Just a little closer.

A sharp pain shot through Oso's leg, jolting him from his reverie. The buck dashed off into the woods before he could release his arrow.

"Time to eat, boy," said one of the reivers. "Now take the bowl this time or I'll break your leg."

Oso stared back at the reiver, hate welling up in his eyes. Still, he took the bowl. He needed to eat, to keep his strength up, otherwise he'd never escape. Oso held the bowl to his nose, sniffing at the contents. Some kind of stew, he decided. It didn't smell very good, but he really didn't have a choice. He gobbled it down quickly. His stomach growled for more, but he doubted he'd get any. Thomas had also finished his meal, and now lay back against the tree. His eyes closed, Oso wondered if he actually slept.

"No, just resting," said Thomas.

"How did you know—"

"It was nothing," said Thomas, opening his eyes and leaning forward. He quickly examined what was going on around them. The reivers had formed their camp in a circle, with the tree as its center. Eight reivers guarded them. Either Killeran was a wary man or one frightened easily by two boys. "It seems that we are quite popular this evening."

"Yes, it does seem that way, doesn't it," said Oso. "We should be honored, I guess, having eight nursemaids." Oso's voice rose so the guards could hear. "Two boys and eight nursemaids."

Though every part of him hurt, Oso knew what Thomas was thinking. Escape. He was thinking it as well. But they wouldn't succeed if eight guards stood around them all night. Maybe some would grow bored with their duty, and Oso's words would be remembered. Some of the reivers might find something better to do than guard two boys and slip away for a few hours, giving them a chance.

"Remarkable, isn't it," said Thomas. "We're tied to a tree by our necks, and our arms and legs are chained together, yet still we garner this much attention. You know, Oso, we really should be honored."

The guards didn't appear to be paying attention to them, but Thomas knew that they could hear their chatter. They might be wasting their time in idle conversation at the moment, but they had nothing to lose. Besides, it might work. Fewer eyes meant more of a chance at freedom.

"Stop the chatter or you'll be dead boys," said Kursool, who came striding toward them from the direction of Killeran's tent. The sergeant was a broad man. Thomas judged that with his massive shoulders he was wide enough for two men. As a result, his legs looked tiny, which made his whole body appear disproportionate.

The sergeant stopped right in front of them. Unexpectedly, he lashed out with his leg, striking Oso across the chin. The blow sent him reeling. The only thing that kept him from falling to the grass was the chain around his neck. Oso fought against the pain, the blow having reawakened all of his injuries earned during his early morning struggle with the reivers. He refused to cry out, though. He would not show any sign of weakness to this bastard. Slowly, he pulled himself back up, until he lay back against the trunk. If not for the tree, he wouldn't have had the strength to hold himself up.

Kursool nodded in satisfaction, pleased with the effects of his blow. He then turned his attention to the other boy and was about to deliver another kick when his eyes caught Thomas'. It was full dark now and Thomas' eyes glowed brightly. They resembled green fire, mirroring the anger contained within him. The sergeant knew what Thomas was thinking. He knew it in his heart. If the boy was free, the sergeant would already be dead. Kursool was not accustomed to fear. He had seen much in his life, having fought in many campaigns, but he had never seen anything like this. He took a step back from the tree.

"You," he said, motioning to one of the reivers standing guard. "Unlock the small one. Lord Killeran wants to see him." The reiver rushed forward, eager to do the sergeant's bidding. He twisted the key in the lock holding the chain around Thomas' neck, then pulled him to his feet. Thomas realized that his plans for escape would have to wait. As the sergeant and the reiver dragged him across the ground, a sense of foreboding filled him.

4

AN UNWANTED MEETING

Kursool and the reiver dropped Thomas like a sack of potatoes on the thick carpet that blanketed the floor of the tent, giving him a quick kick to the gut to punctuate his displeasure at having to drag him. After weathering the blow, Thomas examined his new surroundings with a careful eye. The furnishings were luxurious, especially for a field tent.

A dozen or more rugs were piled one on top of the other to cover the grass. A large cot sat to one side. Costly sheets and blankets lay atop it. At the foot of the bed sat a large leather trunk. Off to the other side was a small table, yet one so ornately carved it looked remarkably out of place. Four matching chairs stood around the table. The entire set of furniture must have been several hundred years old.

Thomas studied the different pieces, his eyes running over the curling spokes that formed the backs of the chairs. The style was familiar. Searching his memory, it didn't take him long to place the origin of the furniture. Highland woodworking. Thomas tasted the bile rising in the back of his throat and felt the anger coursing within his veins. Stolen from the Highlands. He had promised his grandfather that he would protect the Highlands and its people. Yet, a foreign army marauded through the countryside, killing his people and destroying his homeland. And he had done barely anything about it. His ire grew stronger, in addition to his shame. He imagined his grandfather looking at him now, the disappointment clear in his eyes.

Thomas pushed those thoughts away, thoughts that plagued him ever since he learned how to fight and use the Talent. Rynlin and Rya knew of the charges given to him by Talyn. They had told him many times before that he was not ready yet to make good on his responsibilities. It was getting harder and harder for him to listen to their advice. Soon, very soon, he would return, and then—

"So the hero remains defiant, even when covered in blood and dirt," said Killeran as he strode into the tent. He unhooked the clasp around his throat and threw his cloak on the bed, then pulled off his gloves and dropped them on the small table. Someone had cleaned the mud and dirt from his armor, polishing it anew. The breastplate gleamed brightly in the candlelight.

Thomas watched the large-nosed lord closely, examining his movements, his habits, anything he might be able to use against him.

Killeran walked around his prisoner slowly, hands clasped behind his back, his boots sinking into the thick rugs. He laughed softly to himself. "Normally I wouldn't bother with one such as you," he said, circling Thomas much like a shark did its prey. "You'd be dead or begging to be put to work in the mines for what you did. But you intrigue me."

Killeran stopped in front of Thomas, staring down at the boy. Hard green eyes stared back, sending a chill down his spine. Killeran almost took a step back, but he stopped himself, his courage fortified by the chains around the boy's ankles and wrists. He cleared his throat, trying to regain his composure, while pushing down the speck of fear that entered his heart.

This boy was dangerous, more dangerous than he originally thought. Killeran had shrugged off his capture by the boy as a stroke of luck. Now he wasn't so sure.

"There is much I would like to know about you. If you answer my questions, then perhaps it will only be the mines for you." As images of the boy working in the mines popped into his head, Killeran regained more of his confidence. "If not, then you will die slowly and painfully. The choice is up to you."

Thomas' face darkened, his green eyes blazing. This time Killeran did step back. Thomas noticed that Killeran had several nervous habits. When he was unsure of himself, he squeezed his eyes tighter together, scrunching up his face. That, and his large nose, enhanced his resemblance to a rat. He also had the tendency of crossing one arm across his stomach while cupping his chin in his other hand and tapping his fingers on his upper lip just below his nose. Even in a position of power, Killeran was still nervous, perhaps even scared. Thomas' expression became harder.

"What's your name boy?"

Thomas remained silent, kneeling in front of Killeran, his face a mask.

"I said, what's your name, boy?" Killeran repeated. "Where are you from?"

Killeran waited a few moments for a response. "Why did you help the Highlanders? You certainly don't look like one of them."

Thomas refused to speak, though his eyes were locked on Killeran's.

Killeran sighed in mock exasperation. "I thought it might come to this." The pleasure in his voice was obvious, which worried Thomas.

Killeran walked over to the small table and poured himself a glass of red wine from a gold pitcher. He took a sip from the flagon before he picked up a pair of gloves. Metal studs laced the outside of each glove, the fingers left open.

"Do you know what these are, boy?" Killeran asked, taking another sip from his wine. He didn't bother to give him time to answer. "No, I didn't think so." He stood in front of Thomas again, holding his hands before him.

"These are cestus, boy. Boxers used them hundreds, maybe even thousands, of years ago. You see, back then, things weren't as civilized. Now, during a boxing match, when someone is knocked unconscious, or severely injured, the fight is stopped and a winner declared. Of course, the boxers only use their hands, not cestus."

Killeran circled Thomas again, enjoying the sound of his own voice. "But centuries ago, boxing matches were decided in a slightly different way. They were often fought to the death, and the cestus were very useful for breaking someone's bones. As we do today, betting on boxing matches was a profitable business. Today, the winner is either obvious or picked by a judge. But before the sport became more civilized, it was often difficult to determine the winner, because in some matches both boxers died. So they counted how many bones had been broken. The one with the fewest broken bones won, posthumously of course."

Killeran laughed wickedly. "Now let's start over. What's your name, boy?"

Killeran stopped behind Thomas, who still refused to answer. There was no reason to make things easy for Killeran. No reason at all.

"I said, what's your name, boy?" A flash of pain shot through Thomas as he landed face down on the rug, the back of his head throbbing from Killeran's blow. Killeran yanked him back to a kneeling position with the collar around his neck. "What's your name, boy?"

This time Thomas didn't even have the chance to answer.

Killeran struck him again, this time on the side of the head where he had been hit earlier in the day. He toppled to the floor in agony. Killeran let him lie there this time.

"You see, boy, being difficult is really no help to anyone — you or me. If you answer my questions, it will go much more smoothly between us."

Killeran's voice was calm and reassuring. Thomas ignored it. Spots danced in front of his eyes, and he couldn't see straight. Worst of all, his head wouldn't stop spinning. He thought he was going to be sick, but he refused to give Killeran the satisfaction.

"Now, let's move on to another subject." Killeran began pacing in front of him. "You have a very unique fighting style. One that surprised me at first. You see, I'm a student of combat, yet you fought in a way I had never seen before. In many ways you fought like a Marcher would, in others you assumed a style of fighting that I've never seen before. In fact, for a time I thought you were fighting like a Carthanian would, and that civilization disappeared thousands of years ago. Where did you learn to fight like that?"

Killeran's voice almost begged for Thomas' answer. The force of Killeran's kick into Thomas' stomach forced him over onto his back. He lay there trying to catch his breath, and it was several moments before he finally tasted air again. Thomas wanted to curl up into a ball and wish his pain away, but he gritted his teeth instead, focusing on what he would do when he escaped.

Killeran walked back to the table and took another sip from his goblet of wine. "I see it's going to be a long night." The thought didn't displease him.

In the next few hours, Thomas learned what the ancient boxers must have felt like after a fight. He thought after being dragged behind the column for the entire day his body could never hurt so much. He was wrong. Eventually, he was able to close his mind to the pain and actually withdraw from his body somewhat. His mind grew numb under Killeran's onslaught and he lost track of time, hovering on the brink of unconsciousness.

Finally, after what seemed like days but was only hours, Killeran tired of his sport and called for the guards, who picked up Thomas by the arms and dragged him back toward the tree. As he left the tent, Killeran's final words echoed painfully in Thomas' head: "You will talk, boy. It's just a matter of time, but you will talk."

5
______

A PACT

Though Oso's exhaustion consumed him, he couldn't sleep. The chain around his neck holding him to the tree was only part of the reason. His worry for his new friend dominated his thoughts. They had taken Thomas away hours before, and every second that passed became more nerve-wracking for him. Oso owed his life to Thomas. If not for him, the women and children of his village would be with him right now. His having to work in the mines was one thing. He could deal with that. He might even survive for a time, and possibly even escape, though the odds of doing so were slim. No one had ever escaped from the mines before, except by dying.

However, the thought that he had failed in his responsibility, that the women and children would die underground because of him, was something he could not bear. Thomas saved him from that — the shame, the recrimination. Now Oso owed Thomas a debt, yet he couldn't repay it. Not now. Not chained to a tree like an animal.

For the hundredth time he glanced toward Killeran's tent. Each time before, he had hoped to see Thomas emerge. Yet each time he had not, and his worry and anger increased. Oso sat up a little straighter. He thought he saw movement around the tent's entrance. A few minutes later dark shadows moved toward him, their identities hidden by the night. After Thomas' raid the night before, Killeran had not allowed any fires. He was afraid there might be more like Thomas out in the forest somewhere. The shadows eventually took shape, and Oso saw the sergeant and the reiver making their way to the tree with Thomas hanging limply between them.

The two reivers roughly threw Thomas back against the tree. Oso's new friend looked horrible. Thomas' face was swollen along one jaw, with a large bruise over his right eye. A cut above his left eye dripped blood slowly down the side of his face to fall onto his torn shirt. And those were only the obvious injuries. Oso was afraid of what he might find in the morning, when the sunlight exposed everything Killeran had done to Thomas. His friend appeared oblivious to what was going on around him as he slumped against the tree. The reiver forced his head back against the bark and strung the chain through Thomas' collar.

A white-hot rage welled up in Oso. He tested his chains for the hundredth time, lunging forward in an effort to get at the reiver. The chains held, much as Oso had expected. Still, it felt good to try.

"Don't like what Lord Killeran did to your friend?" asked the reiver, laughing softly under his breath. "Well, you'll get your turn. Don't worry about that." The sounds of laughter drifted off into the night, following the footsteps of the two reivers as they headed for their bedrolls.

Oso waited several minutes before talking, unsure of what to say. He felt responsible for what had happened to Thomas. He should have been the one to experience Killeran's wrath, not Thomas. The shame that Thomas had helped him avoid with the women and children took hold of him nonetheless.

"Are you all right, Thomas?"

Thomas took a few moments to answer. The pounding in his head echoed through his entire body. "I will be." Thomas' voice was a whisper. If he spoke any louder it would only exacerbate the pounding.

"I'm sorry, Thomas. This is my fault. If not for me, you wouldn't be in this situation. You should have let me die."

Thomas chuckled softly, ignoring the pain that ran through his body in waves. "We will get out of this together, Oso. Blaming yourself won't help."

"But—"

"No buts, Oso." Thomas' voice was stern, and louder than he intended. His head felt like it was going to split in two. "I made the choice to help. You didn't make it for me."

"Thomas, if I had not failed in my responsibility to the village—"

"Oso, are you trying to take away my ability to choose?" asked Thomas in anger. "If you take away that, you take away my freedom."

"No, not at all," Oso replied. He was confused. He was trying to apologize. Why was Thomas getting angry? "I was just trying to apologize."

"No, you weren't," said Thomas. "You were trying to blame yourself for what happened, and by doing that you were taking away my choice. There is no reason for you to apologize. Is that understood?"

Oso nodded, then realized Thomas might not be able to see him in the darkness. "Yes."

"Good." Thomas placed his head gently against the bark, taking a few deep breaths. He tried to block away the pain as best he could. "Sometimes the only freedom a person has is the ability to choose, whether it's a particular course of action or something as simple as what to have for dinner. If you take away that choice, you take away that person's freedom. If you don't have your freedom, you have nothing."

Oso sat staring at the shadow of his friend for a long time. His friend's words banked the fire of his anger. Thomas fell asleep soon afterwards. Oso couldn't sleep. Thomas' words kept running through his mind, especially one: freedom. He had always thought of himself as free, even if the reivers occupied part of the Highlands. But was he truly free? By morning, he had still not found an answer.

6

____

A NEW HOME

The next few days were much like the first for Thomas and Oso, and their shared hardships only served to bring them closer as friends. A bond began to form between them, a bond that grew stronger with each step. Neither had a brother growing up. Now it felt like they did.

During the day they continued to walk behind the last two reivers in the column, most of their attention focused on the ground in front of them. They had gotten better at it, so much so that by the fourth day they had mastered the skill and rarely fell down anymore, though the thought of being dragged behind the horses for a short time as a brief respite did appeal to them from time to time.

The nights were harder. For Oso, he had to sit in silence against the tree as the reivers took into Killeran's tent, and then a few hours later dragged him out. Killeran was very good at what he was doing, making sure he didn't break any bones. But that didn't prevent him from inflicting a great deal of pain.

The second night, after Thomas' latest ordeal, Oso asked what Killeran was doing to him and why. In a mechanical voice, Thomas replayed the events of the past few hours, explaining how Killeran began with the cestus and then moved on to the flail. Eventually Killeran grew bored with trying to beat information out of him and let him go for the night.

The story chilled Oso's heart. He couldn't understand how his friend could endure so much. Yet he had. Night after night. Though Thomas had ordered Oso not to blame himself, he could not rid himself of the guilt that plagued him. However, instead of letting the guilt sit within his heart and fester, he used it for a more positive purpose, promising himself that when the time came to repay his debt to Thomas, he would be ready.

Thomas actually began to enjoy the days. At least then any pain he felt was inflicted by his own carelessness. Killeran succeeded only in finding out Thomas' name, and that because a reiver heard Oso call him that when they were talking one night. After a while, Killeran hadn't bothered to ask questions. He only wanted to inflict pain, taking a sadistic pleasure in the task.

Thomas hated Killeran. He hated him more than he had ever hated anything or anyone in his life. After that first night in Killeran's tent, and having to feel those cestus pound into his body again and again, he swore to himself that one day Killeran would die a slow, painful death. Every night thereafter he swore the oath. Sometimes it was the only thing that kept him from breaking.

On the evening of the fourth day, as the sun slowly slid behind the mountaintops, the column of reivers finally rode into a small valley surrounded on three sides by steep cliffs. Where the valley narrowed Killeran had constructed a large, square wooden palisade. Watch towers stood on each corner made of stone connected to a thirty-foot-high wall constructed from the stoutest trees in the Highlands. A ditch filled with wooden spikes surrounded the fort, with just enough space between the two to allow his soldiers to shoot anyone foolish enough to come too close.

Within the compound were Killeran's private quarters, barracks for his soldiers and the slave pens. At times he thought it was all a bit much when he considered the power exercised by his warlocks, as no sane Highlander would come near the walls. Of course, at times he doubted the sanity of the Highlanders with their never-ending desire to disrupt his plans.

"So how do you two like your new home?" asked Killeran, who had ridden back from the head of the column. The boys' expressions were the same — hard, flinty, filled with malice.

Killeran laughed. They could dream of whatever they wanted now, even his death, but once they were in the mines they would think of little else but their own deaths.

"Sergeant, escort these two to the cells beneath the barracks. I don't want them mixed with the other workers yet."

"Yes, sir."

As Killeran rode triumphantly into his fortress, the sergeant and a few reivers prodded Thomas and Oso through the gates. It looked very much like they had expected. There were two large barracks, one built next to the outer walls, the other parallel to it that served as the reivers' quarters. Another barracks, on the other side of the fort, and a good distance away from the other two, must be for the warlocks. No sane man would stay near a warlock any closer than necessary. A smaller barracks, which resembled a quaint cabin, they quickly discovered to be Killeran's, as he threw his reins to a guard and strode up the steps into his quarters. Then they saw the cages.

Near the warlocks' barracks, running along the outer palisade, were five steel pens. They resembled the cages used when tracking dangerous animals, but were built on a much larger scale.

Thomas and Oso stopped dead in their tracks, unable to

take their eyes from them. They were filled with people, a few to the point where there was barely any room to sit or lie down. The slave pens. Both Thomas and Oso had heard of them, but no one who had ever seen them had escaped from the fort before.

The sight sickened them. The people were dirty and unkempt, and obviously undernourished. Their clothes were nothing more than rags. A tear came to Thomas' eye. There were children in the cages, many children, and they looked to be doing the worst of all.

The sergeant poked them from behind with the butt of his spear, forcing Thomas and Oso forward. He directed them to the reivers' barracks. As they passed closer to the slave pens, Thomas averted his eyes. He couldn't bear to look. The pain he had endured during the past four days was nothing compared to what he experienced now. What shocked him the most upon seeing the Highlanders in the cages was not their appearance, but rather their manner.

The most distinguishing characteristic of any Highlander was attitude. They held a confidence in themselves unseen in many other lands. Not arrogance, but a quiet belief in their abilities and in their Kingdom. Now, their eyes were dull and held no life, the confidence stolen. Nothing was there, not even hope.

And it was his fault. He was the Lord of the Highlands, or would be, and he had done nothing to help these people. Nothing at all. He had stayed safely on the Isle of Mist while his people, the people he was responsible for, suffered. Guilt rushed into him, filling up every pore and crevice within his body. He was ashamed of who he was. He was ashamed at what his grandfather would say if he could see what had happened. He was ashamed most of all of himself, and he didn't think anything he did in the future could ever take that shame away.

7

THE MINES

The day after arriving at Killeran's compound, Thomas and Oso entered the mines. Killeran hoped that the experience would soften the green-eyed boy, since his attempts during the journey had failed. There were other things besides pain that would serve Killeran's purpose, many of which could be found hundreds of feet below ground.

The smoky torches struggled in vain against the encroaching darkness. Spaced one hundred feet apart on the roughly cut wall, they were no more than pinpricks in a sea of black. To the miners, though, light or dark was of little consequence. You worked more with your hands than your eyes.

The dreariness and hopelessness of the mines immediately pushed Thomas into planning an escape, he had nothing else to think about while hammering away at the rock. Unfortunately, any path he chose was fraught with one guarantee. He would have to deal with the warlocks.

Yet, the plan that he formed during the monotonous, endless hours of black drudgery was much more ambitious than simply he and Oso escaping. He would not leave this place until every Highlander here did so before him. During the first night in his cell beneath the reivers' barracks, Thomas did a much better job of torturing himself than Killeran ever had. The faces of the Highlanders he had seen upon entering the fort — the sad, lost looks; the resignation in their eyes — continually played through his mind. He lay on the hard stone floor in a cold sweat, and when he finally did fall asleep a few hours before dawn, he would have preferred to stay awake.

The face of a small boy popped into his dreams. He was lying on his side up against the steel bars, looking out at what was going on in the fort. The vitality expected in a child was missing from his eyes. He should have been smiling and playing with his friends on the village green. Instead he was locked in a cage, covered in dirt and eating watery soup for his only meal of the day.

In the dream, the boy stared at Thomas for what seemed like days, but this time the eyes were alive — with accusation. He knew that he was in the cage because of Thomas. The boy was much too weak to even voice his thoughts. Yet his eyes spoke for him: *Why? Why do you let them keep me here?* Thomas didn't know how to answer.

That nightmare gave way to another, of an old woman cradling a crying child in her arms. She too rested against the steel bars, using them to support her aching back. The woman wouldn't last in the mines much longer, and she knew it. The girl wasn't her daughter, but there was no one else in the cage who could care for her. Her mother had died earlier in the day. She had given her daughter part of her daily ration to keep her strong, but it had only hastened her own demise. The old woman raised her head to meet his watching eyes. He knew what she was thinking: *We die and you do nothing. Why?*

The last vision soon followed. Thomas stood by the entrance to the mines at the edge of the pit, the dumping ground for those who died in the mines. He looked down at the corpse of a Highlander, a man who had probably once been a

Marcher. The buzzards and crows had not yet ravaged his body. The Highlander had died a few hours before, the mines having slowly worn away his will to live, and having already claimed his wife. He had nothing to live for, nothing to hope for. Thomas stared down at the dead man for a long time, a deep sadness settling into his bones. He felt older than his seventeen years, but no wiser nor stronger.

Much to his surprise, as he was about to turn away, the corpse rose to a sitting position and turned its head toward Thomas. The eyes remained lifeless and cold. "I would have fought for you," the dead Highlander said in a raspy tone. "I would have died for you. But instead I died for nothing. Where have you been?"

Thomas woke up shivering that morning, drenched in his own sweat. The reivers came soon after that, taking him from his cell and leading him up into the dawn to join Oso and a hundred other Highlanders on the short trek to the mines. They exited through the main gate, one reiver for every worker, then followed a steep, sloping path that went down into the foothills below the fort. The entrance to the mines appeared before him, the hole resembling the gaping maw of some beast.

Thomas followed the man in front of him, pulled on by the chains around his ankles and neck. Glancing to his left, he saw the pit he had dreamed of, exactly as he had seen it in his sleep. Thankfully, a Marcher did not lie atop it — not yet anyway. As he trudged through the mine entrance, the oppressiveness of the tons of stone pushing down on him from above almost overwhelmed him.

It took more than an hour for the Highlanders to reach their destination in the bowels of the earth, walking carefully on the treacherous path. The mountain was silent, except for the tread of feet on the rocky floor and the occasional curse by a reiver and the slash of a whip, urging a Highlander to move faster. The Highlanders didn't talk in the mines. Every word said equaled one lash.

Finally they reached their destination, a small side tunnel that branched off from the main passageway. Thomas guessed that they were at least a mile beneath the surface. One by one the reivers unchained the Highlanders from their leg shackles, then led them farther into the darkness barely held back by the torches hanging from the wall. Soon a reiver came for Thomas. He was taken down a side tunnel for several minutes until the reiver told him to stop. He heard the Highlanders ahead of him already working. The sharp clang of their pickaxes striking the rock echoed down the passageway.

The reiver pulled a chain up from the floor of the tunnel and attached it to the shackle around Thomas' neck. He tugged on the chain where it met the rock to ensure that the metal spike was still firmly attached to the stone. Satisfied that it was, he handed Thomas his pick and told him to start digging. If anything shined in the light, dig it out and place it in the bucket at his feet.

Thomas stood there for several minutes, examining his current plight. The darkness didn't bother him. His eyes allowed him to see quite well in the mines. Yet, he could understand how it affected the spirit of someone who could not see so clearly in the dark. The darkness whittled away at a person's spirit, until there was nothing left but the sound of the pickaxe striking the stone. In time, even that wouldn't be enough, and the person's essence would gradually seep away, and with it the will to live.

With nothing else to do, he went to work. The hours passed slowly, and Thomas was in no rush to accomplish his task. Refusing to work served no purpose at all and could easily end in his death. Instead, he used the time to clear his mind of the shame and guilt that had plagued him for the last few days. He had failed his people. He wasn't there when they needed him.

Though he could do nothing about the past, he could do something about their present situation.

He spent most of the day figuring out how to escape, but not just him and Oso. No, when he left this place, he was going to take all the Highlanders with him. That would help atone for his failure to a certain extent. Then he could focus on driving Killeran and his reivers out of the Highlands once and for all. It soon became clear to him that there was only one way to do that. But he would worry about that later, focusing on the task at hand.

A reiver walked by every so often, checking Thomas' bucket. Thomas had found a few pieces of gold, but he threw those farther down the tunnel, instead filling the bucket with iron ore. He would work in the mines as long as necessary, but he refused to turn a profit for Killeran. In the beginning, his body ached in protest and his head pounded with each swing of the pickaxe, his tortured muscles screaming out in pain. Yet, as time passed, the activity worked the kinks out of his muscles and in a way rejuvenated him.

The last time the reiver came he unleashed Thomas and led him back to the other miners. When he finally returned to the surface, he was surprised to see that it was almost full dark, having completely lost track of the time while beneath the ground. But his day had not been wasted. He had developed an escape plan. All it would require was a little patience and luck, but first he wanted to talk with Oso.

Thomas and the others trudged wearily back up the steep trail, many barely able to walk. Once they reached the camp the Highlanders returned to the cages while Oso and Thomas were escorted to their cells. As he was pushed roughly back into his new home, Thomas smiled. His plan would work if he waited for the right time. Now, he just had to make sure he was still alive when it was time to act.

8

TOSSING THE CABER

"I don't know how I'm going to do it, Thomas," Oso whispered fiercely. "But I'm going to kill that bastard Killeran if I have to do it with my bare hands."

They were alone in the basement, which was divided into four cells by steel bars. The cells were empty, as the reivers had made it a point to remove the straw normally used for beds. The only light came through a small window covered by a metal grille set high in the wall. To look outside, they had to pull themselves up the steel bars of their cells. They could then see the main courtyard with Killeran's quarters to one side and the warlocks' barracks across the muddy common ground.

"You'll have to get in line, Oso," said Thomas. "I'm sure that besides us, there are several hundred other Highlanders who also want a crack at him."

Oso laughed softly. The swelling on his face had gone down, and despite the strenuous activity required in the mines, the wound on his arm no longer bothered him. "You're probably right about that." He, too, had been greatly affected by what the reivers had done to his people. The fact that he could do nothing about it at the moment gnawed at him constantly.

Neither saw each other during the day. Thomas was always at the front of the line of workers, while Oso was in the back. When they returned to their cells after a day in the mines, a small bowl of watery gruel always sat waiting on the floor for them, hours cold. They dug into the slop hungrily, eating in silence. And each night they became restless, pacing around their small cells in frustration.

Thomas decided to wait before he told Oso his plan for escaping. There was no reason to give him a sense of false hope, and he didn't know how long he would have to wait for the right circumstances. It was a very simple plan, really, but one that depended on a key variable over which Thomas had no control. He'd have to watch and wait, and be ready to strike when the time was right.

"So how do the Highlanders stand now against the reivers?" asked Thomas.

His question served two purposes. First, he wanted to change the subject, as he could see that Oso was getting worked up over their current predicament. He hadn't known his new friend for long, but he had learned much about him in that short span of time. One of Oso's primary characteristics was the need for action. If something needed to be done, he wanted to do it, and right away.

Unfortunately, what Oso wanted to accomplish at the moment was all but impossible, yet his need for action demanded that he do something. So he walked around his cell and pounded his palm with a fist. Second, Thomas wanted to find out more about his people since he had been away from them for so long.

Oso sighed. He knew that his anger was useless, but it was very difficult for him to let things go. "Some have accepted defeat and think only of their own survival. Others continue the struggle." Oso stopped pacing and looked at Thomas, though he continued to pound his fist into his palm, the smack echoing in the small basement. "Were you raised in the Highlands?"

"For a time."

"Then you know what it is to be a Highlander?" Oso's question had many underlying meanings.

"Yes, I do."

Highlanders were warriors, and had been for millennia. To hear that some had given up the struggle disheartened him. Even when there was no chance of victory, throughout the centuries Highlanders had refused to surrender. Accepting defeat went against their very nature.

Oso nodded. "Those who have given up are few. Most of us still fight, though we don't have the resources to challenge Killeran directly. In any normal battle, yes, we could defeat him, though the casualties would be high. But we rarely have the opportunity to fight a normal battle."

Thomas understood. No one could challenge the mastery of the Highlanders on the battlefield when fighting with conventional weapons, such as a sword or spear. Killeran had an advantage that the Highlanders could not defend against — the warlocks. The only way to stand against the Dark Magic of the warlocks was to combat it with a power of their own, but the Highlanders had no one with such skill. The last Highland sorcerers had died during the Great War.

"Another problem," said Oso, "is that we don't have a leader. When the Lord of the Highlands died, there was no one to take his place. His son was murdered and the grandson disappeared. Some say the grandson still lives, but more likely he's been dead for years. As a result, the leader of each village up in the higher passes rules as best as he or she can, but none have the ability to bring the Marchers together again and make the Highlands one. Most are simply concerned about survival. It is a very difficult situation."

Thomas' heart clenched when Oso mentioned his grandfather. He was glad that Oso couldn't see his face in the dim light of the basement. A wave of guilt broke against his resolve, and the shame he had held back during the day while working in the mines flooded across the mental barrier he had constructed. His failure rose up to confront him once again.

His grandfather had left him with several tasks to accomplish right before he died. Thomas knew that the only way to remove the shame and guilt once and for all was to complete those tasks. Until then, he would continue to mentally whip himself. But could he accomplish them? Self-doubt plagued him.

"If a leader was found, would they fight?"

Oso thought for a moment before answering. "Yes, we would fight."

That was a start at least. If Thomas could rally the Highlanders, his chances for succeeding would be that much greater. Still, when it was time to reclaim his grandfather's title, he certainly would have his work cut out for him.

"Right now, though, I can think of only one person who could lead us," said Oso, pacing around the small cell again. Thomas watched him in silence. "As I said, it is rumored that the grandson survived, and many still believe it, if only because it gives them hope. If we are to regain our freedom, we need the Lost Kestrel. Of course, as I said, he probably met the same fate as his father and grandfather, but who can say. At the moment, hope is our only ally. Unfortunately, as time passes, even our hope dies."

"You never know, Oso. You never know."

"You're right about that, Thomas. You never know. But until I see this Lost Kestrel with my own eyes—" He leaned against the wall of his cell. "Well, hope is a good thing, I guess. Especially when you have nothing else."

"Skepticism is a good thing, too," said Thomas. He had learned what he wanted, so he decided to change the conversation once again. Their talking so far had been serious, and in some ways discouraging. Their cells were bleak enough. "How did you get your nickname?"

Oso settled down against the wall. A smile appeared on his face, and he finally stopped pounding his fist into his palm.

"From time to time, some of the villages gather together. It's very much like a fair, such as the great Eastern Festival at the border of Dunmoor and Fal Carrach, though on a much smaller scale. We have vendors and hawkers, dancing and sporting events." From Oso's voice, Thomas gathered that his friend enjoyed the last the most. "One of the competitions is tossing the caber. You throw a pole as far as you can."

"That sounds simple enough," said Thomas.

"In concept, yes. Actually doing it is another matter. The pole is about thirty feet long and two hands wide. Trying to balance the thing is almost impossible. You hold it with two hands at the bottom, so it's sticking straight up in the air, and you rest its weight on your shoulder. Then you try to run up to the line without dropping it or hurting yourself and then heave it." Oso laughed with pleasure.

"That can't be very hard at all," said Thomas.

"Yes, well—" Oso looked through the bars at his friend, who sat across from him in the dim light. Thomas' green eyes sparkled with mischief. "Thank you for the sarcasm."

"My pleasure."

"Anyway, when I was thirteen, I tried it for the first time and I won. I beat men who were bigger than me and two or three times my age. It was the most fun I've ever had." Thomas saw that his friend was flushed with pride. For the moment, Oso had forgotten their present circumstances. "One of the men I beat was named Coban. He came over to congratulate me after the contest. He said I was as strong as a bear. Someone else overheard and gave me the nickname Oso, from the old tongue. It's stuck with me ever since."

"Coban, you said?" asked Thomas. "Coban Serenan?"

"Yes, you know him?" Oso leaned forward in surprise, suddenly curious.

"Yes, I do," said Thomas. "You said that this contest was when you were thirteen, so it was after the fall of the Crag."

"Yes, it was."

Thomas sighed with relief, a huge smile crossing his face. He had assumed that everyone in the Crag had died. If Coban fought his way free, others probably did as well.

"Yes, I know Coban, but I haven't seen him since I was a small child. I knew him at the Crag."

Oso sensed that his friend had lost interest in conversing. He was somewhere else, probably living in his memories. Oso desperately wanted to know why Thomas had been at the Crag. Had he been there during the attack? Who else did he know? But he didn't ask. It just didn't seem like the right time. Maybe later.

Coban was one of the few Marchers who had escaped from the Crag, and he and the other survivors refused to talk about it. The memories were too painful for them. Oso knew that they blamed themselves for what had happened to the Highlands since the death of Talyn Kestrel. He also knew that they had done everything they could to protect the Highland Lord, yet fate had worked against them. And now his new friend had also lived at the Crag. Thomas certainly was full of surprises. He couldn't wait to see what he learned next.

9

FIGHTING BACK

Thomas' days in the mines seemed to last forever. During the day the only sounds that traveled through the tunnels were the rattling of chains, the occasional clunk of a piece of rock dropped into the bucket, and the constant hammering of the pickaxe into the stone. He saw little of the sun, moving from one darkness to the next, with little to amuse himself except thoughts of escape.

Killeran had not yet led another raiding party in search of new workers, so the warlocks remained in the camp. Until Killeran did, and took the majority of warlocks with him, Thomas would have to wait before putting his plan into action.

Of course, Thomas did have to thank the mines for one blessing. Killeran had lost interest in him since he had been put to work, which allowed his body to heal. The cuts and bruises slowly healed, along with the headaches. He had passed the pit at the mine entrance ten mornings, and each time it had been empty — until today, when the body of a small child lay atop the open grave.

The power of the Talent rushed within him for the first time in weeks as he entertained thoughts of killing every reiver in the fort, but it would serve no purpose. The surprise on the face of the child who had died the night before, of not understanding what was going on and why it was happening to him, haunted Thomas throughout the day. There was so much he could do, yet so little. As a result, his rage boiled just beneath the surface, fueled by his frustration, waiting to explode.

Thomas heard the clanking of chains off in the distance and realized his eleventh day in the mines was almost over. The reivers were forming up the chain gang for the slow trip back to the Black Hole, as the Highlanders called Killeran's fort.

A reiver soon appeared before Thomas, walking confidently down the dark tunnel with a key in his hand. Thomas had known of his approach for some time, his bad breath having preceded him. The thought of killing the man with his pickaxe sped across Thomas' mind, but first he'd have to break the chain connecting it to the stone.

The reivers had done everything possible to eliminate any hope for escape. After Thomas put down the pickaxe and stepped away from it so it wasn't within easy reach, the reiver unlocked the chain from Thomas' steel collar and pushed him back up the passageway toward the other miners.

As he drew closer, something looked out of place, something that only he could see in the murky darkness. Normally, the Highlanders stood silently one behind the other once the reivers were ready to go back, exhausted by their efforts. But there was some kind of commotion at the back of the line. Freed from his neck irons, Thomas ran forward, surprising the reiver behind him. The guard shouted for him to stop.

Thomas ignored the reiver, running as fast as he could with the chains still attached to his ankle irons. Thanks to the journey after his capture, he had learned how to move quickly when impeded in such a way. The Highlander at the back of the line was lay on the hard stone floor, curled up into a ball as two reivers viciously kicked him with their steel-tipped boots.

The other Highlanders, chained as they were, could do nothing to help. The Highlander was a threat to no one in his current condition, yet the reivers continued to kick him, their heavy boots thudding into his body.

Thomas lunged toward the two reivers, knocking both of them down. The reivers never expected an attack. Thomas took the opportunity to inflict some punishment of his own. Though his legs were chained, his arms were free. As one of the reivers tried to sit up, Thomas hit him with a flurry of punches. The crunching sound of the man's nose breaking filled Thomas with satisfaction. The anger that had simmered within him during the day finally had a release. The reiver fell back again in pain, clutching at his face as blood poured down onto his shirt.

The second reiver was tangled in the chains around Thomas ankles and having a hard time regaining his feet. Thomas kicked out with his feet, taking the man full in the face. Another crunching sound accompanied the blow. With his two opponents no longer in the mood to fight, he crawled over to the fallen Highlander. The man lay face down on the rocky path and hadn't moved since Thomas intervened. Grabbing hold of the Highlander's shirt, he pulled him over onto his back. Thomas drew back in shock. It was the Highlander in his dream. The Highlander who had spoken to him while sitting on top of the pit outside the mines. The Highlander who had died.

Thomas quickly recovered his senses and placed his ear just above the man's mouth. He was breathing. The man wasn't dead after all. Relief surged through him. If he could prevent one dream from becoming reality, perhaps he could do the same thing about the others as well.

However, his victory was short-lived. Thomas suddenly felt a great weight on his back that crushed him against the ground. A half dozen reivers piled onto him, holding him down. Not satisfied that he was subdued, one of the reivers drew his dagger and brought the hilt down sharply across the back of Thomas' head. The darkness around him became more complete as he lost consciousness. The last fleeting thought that passed through his mind was one of pleasure. The Highlander would live, at least for now. The headache he would wake up with was a small price to pay for that.

10

PROMISE OF PAYMENT

Thomas groaned as his eyes adjusted to the bright light from the torches. He remembered working in the mine, but after that everything was a blank. The pain in the back of his head told him what he needed to know. He was getting very tired of being hit there. Very tired. When he tried to sit up, a wave of dizziness washed over him. Fighting against it, he tried to roll over onto his side, but he couldn't. In fact, he couldn't move at all, except for his head.

Lying back, he waited several minutes for the dizziness to pass. During that time he looked at his surroundings as best as he could. He was in some part of the barracks, he guessed. The floor was covered by a thick rug and the walls by rich tapestries, all with a Highland flair. Except for a large chair at one end of the room that resembled a throne, the room was bare. Killeran's quarters. Only he would have stolen so many things from the Highlanders and displayed it all so brazenly.

Finally, as his vision cleared and his headache receded to a dull thumping at the back of his skull, Thomas raised his chin to his chest. He had been strapped to a board, with his arms and legs tied down. Killeran. Killeran must have something planned.

"So young Thomas plays hero once again," said Killeran, striding confidently into the room. His nose looked even larger to Thomas as Killeran leaned over him. "You know, boy, you're almost more trouble than you're worth."

Thomas stared back at him, not saying a word. He flexed his hands against the leather straps, but knew they would hold no matter how much he struggled. One day he would meet Killeran when he was not chained like a beast or strapped to a table, and then this prissy bastard would learn the true meaning of pain. Until then, Thomas would have to suffer through his ministrations. The thought of using the Talent crossed his mind, but he held back.

"Still not speaking to me?" asked Killeran in mock surprise. He walked around the table so all Thomas could see was his head and his large nose directly above his face. "You should be thanking me profusely, you know. Normally I would have had you killed for attacking my men, but I chose not to. Do you know why?"

Killeran waited expectantly for an answer. Thomas knew it was all part of the game Killeran liked to play. He simply waited, staring up at the large nose hovering above him. He knew what was coming next.

"Tight-lipped as always. Well, since you don't want to guess, I'll tell you." Killeran walked back around the table and started pacing along one side of it. "You see, Thomas, you still intrigue me. Why did you help the Highlanders? Only a fool would have done so. Why do you seem so familiar to me, as if I should recognize you? Why do you refuse to say a word?" Killeran didn't bother to give Thomas time to answer.

"I'd like answers to these and a host of other questions, but you refuse to take part in a civilized conversation. You refuse to say anything at all." Thomas focused on the swishing sound of

Killeran's long white cloak as it trailed behind him across the carpet. He had long since learned that there was really no reason to listen to Killeran's constant ramblings. "Maybe that's why I let you live."

Killeran stopped pacing and leaned over Thomas, his nose almost touching Thomas' face. The stench of the onions Killeran had eaten with his dinner threatened to overpower him. "I have always been able to make someone talk. It's just one of my many skills, but you still hold back what you know. You're a challenge, Thomas. And I love challenges. Remain silent as long as you want. As I said before, you'll break. It's just a matter of time. Of course, the longer it takes, the more fun I get to have."

Killeran snapped his fingers as he glided away from the table. Thomas heard the footsteps of someone entering the room, then leaving, but he couldn't see what was going on.

"The cestus didn't seem to bother you," said Killeran from somewhere behind Thomas. He heard the clinking of metal on metal, yet could only guess at what Killeran was doing. "So I decided it was time to try a different approach."

Killeran walked back around the table, standing in front of Thomas' feet. The evil smile on his face sent a shiver of fear through Thomas' body. He held a red-hot poker in front of him like a sword.

"If you answer my questions, Thomas, you won't have to feel the sting of my friend here," said Killeran, waving the poker lazily through the air. "Now, why did you help the High-landers?" Killeran's question came out as a shout.

Thomas balled his hands into fists in preparation. He told himself not to cry out, no matter what. Focusing on Killeran's nose, Thomas' eyes blazed with hatred.

"Ah, well, I had a feeling you'd be difficult."

As Killeran jabbed the hot tip of the poker into Thomas' side, his body jerked involuntarily against the searing pain.

Thomas wanted to cry out, to scream at the top of his lungs. Yet his jaw remained clenched. Killeran jabbed again, and again, and again. Eventually, Thomas lost count and blissfully drifted off into unconsciousness, the smell of burnt flesh tickling his nose.

11

NOTHING FOR FREE

The cold stone of the cell floor felt like a balm, soothing his tortured skin. The reivers had dumped him there as they would the trash in the garbage pit just beyond the walls of the fort.

"Thomas, what the—"

Oso stood gripping the bars of his cell tightly in his hands, the horror obvious in his face. Even in the dim light, the dozens of small burns that dotted Thomas' chest and back flamed angrily. Oso wanted to help his friend, but the bars prevented it.

Thomas relished the cold against his chest. It was like slipping into a cool pool of water, but only half as far as he wanted.

"Just another one of Killeran's games."

Oso's face became a black cloud as his hands tightened on the bars. "That bastard is a dead man." The heat of his voice matched his emotions. "Mark my words, Thomas. He'll die for this. I promise you."

Yet, even to Oso's ears, his words sounded empty. He was in no position to do anything at all. He had never felt so useless.

"As I said before, Oso, you'll probably have to get in line for that."

Thomas carefully rolled over onto his back, recoiling initially from the cold of the floor before sighing with relief. This was much better. While his chest was still cool he could ease the pain scorching his back.

"What did Killeran do, Thomas?"

Thomas closed his eyes, imagining that the waves on the east coast of the Highlands splashed over him. Oh, what he would give to be there right now. The cold of the floor certainly helped. Unfortunately, his chest was beginning to tingle with pain again. It was going to be a very long night.

"This time he grew tired of the cestus, so he decided to use a poker from the fire instead."

Oso winced at the thought, shuddering at the possibility of having to go through such a thing. He couldn't understand how Thomas could speak as if it was nothing at all. Oso sighed with frustration.

"The Highlanders are talking about it, you know."

"Talking about what?"

Thomas adjusted his back slightly, trying to position a burn that was close to his shoulder blade so it would touch the floor. It was wasted effort. His movement only irritated his injuries, the pinpricks erupting all over his angry red skin. He rolled over onto his stomach again.

"About what you did in the mines. All the Highlanders in the cages know about it."

Oso looked at his friend with pride. He had already told some of the miners about how he and Thomas were captured, risking the lash. This latest effort by Thomas only increased their respect for the green-eyed boy.

"Is the man still alive?"

Thomas didn't care about the gossip. He wanted to know if his actions mattered. His memories of the incident had returned to him quickly, as pain had a remarkable knack for clearing the mind.

"Yes, he lives," said Oso with satisfaction. "A little bruised, perhaps, but all right. He's back in one of the cages and some of the women are looking after him. His name is Aric, by the way. He says he's your man for life now. Once again, a debt is owed. You gave him back his life, and it's yours to command."

"That's very kind of him," said Thomas, rolling onto his back again. The floor wasn't helping him as much as it had in the beginning. "But he doesn't have to do that. He needed help, so I helped him. I'm sure he or any of the others would have done the same."

Oso laughed softly. "Well, you'll have a very hard time convincing Aric of that."

Trying to keep a Highlander from making good on a pledge was much like trying to move a mountain with your bare hands. Besides, everyone knew the mountain would be more reasonable than a Highlander.

They passed the next few minutes in silence. Thomas continued to search for a comfortable position, finally deciding that there wasn't one. Instead, he found a place along the wall so he could talk face to face with Oso. His friend's thoughtful expression told him that Oso was struggling with something. The large Highlander was not the type of person who hid his emotions well.

"What's on your mind, Oso?"

"Huh? Oh, nothing really. I was just curious about something, but I wasn't sure if I should ask or not."

"Go ahead," said Thomas. "I don't think I'll be sleeping very much tonight."

Oso laughed softly, amazed at his friend's ability to make a joke in his current condition.

"When you were in the tunnel, and the reivers were beating on Aric, you were free from the neck chain. You could have used it as a diversion and escaped."

"Yes, I guess I could have," said Thomas.

"Then why didn't you?"

Oso thought it was the most logical thing in the world for Thomas to do.

"I don't know," said Thomas, taking a moment to gather his thoughts.

He probably could have escaped then, if he really wanted to. The reivers were too busy with Aric to stop him, and once he was in the side tunnels, he could have easily disappeared until the reivers left. But he hadn't. After spending almost two weeks in this hovel, he wanted to do nothing more than get out. Yet that thought had never crossed his mind when he saw what the reivers were doing to that lone Highlander. Escape had never been an option. His instincts had taken over. The Highlander needed assistance, and he was the only one who could provide it. So he did what he had to do. Rya would have been proud of him.

It really wasn't a very difficult puzzle to solve. He was a member of the Sylvana, and though still rather new to it all, his responsibilities as a Sylvan Warrior had already become a part of who he was: to fight against the evil of the Shadow Lord, to protect the forest and its inhabitants, to help those in need. To not do anything would go against the very essence of his being. He had the added weight of also being a Highlander — the Highland Lord in hiding as Rynlin had joked a few times. These were his people, and whether they knew it or not, it didn't change the duty he had to them

"I guess all I can say is that escaping then would have been wrong."

"What do you mean wrong?" Oso failed to keep the shock from his voice.

"I mean, if I escaped then, without helping Aric, I could only look at myself as a coward. I could have helped, but I chose not to. Instead, I chose to run and possibly gain my free-dom. If I had done that, I don't think I could live with myself."

"That's a very harsh appraisal, Thomas. Most people probably would have tried to escape, and no one would have blamed them for doing so."

"You may be right," agreed Thomas, clenching his teeth briefly as the circles of fire dotting his skin flared up. "But if you hold yourself to the standards of most everyone else, you have little opportunity to improve as a person. My grandmother always says, 'You must do what you must do.' It took me a long time to figure out what she meant, and once I did I fought it for a while. But no matter how hard I tried, I couldn't escape it. You must do what you must do."

Oso stared at Thomas, not sure what to make of his new friend. He spoke as if what he had done was the most natural thing in the world, yet it was anything but.

"You are a unique person, Thomas. I am honored to call you a friend."

"And I you, Oso." Thomas smiled at the compliment. "Besides, I've decided that I won't be taking my leave of our kind and gracious host until everyone here can go with me."

"You mean free everyone?"

"Yes, I do."

Now Oso knew exactly what to make of his new friend — brave, and crazy.

"You don't have to look at me that way, Oso. I haven't lost my mind."

"All right, then, I guess I'll have to reserve judgment. How do you plan to do it?"

Thomas tried to settle himself more comfortably against the stone wall. It was hopeless. He'd simply have to deal with the pain.

"What keeps us here, Oso?"

Oso thought it was a fairly simple question, and answered immediately. "The reivers."

"No, not the reivers, though they play a part. The reason

we're still here, the reason the Highlanders are still here, is the warlocks."

Oso looked as if some hidden meaning had suddenly dawned on him. He was a fool for not seeing it before. It was the exact same reason the Highlanders could not defeat the reivers in battle. They didn't have the weapons needed to fight the warlocks.

"So we need to eliminate the warlocks." It was the most obvious solution, but Oso's high spirits quickly deflated. It was also an impossible one.

"Yes, we do," said Thomas with quiet confidence.

Oso almost laughed. His friend must have been hit on the head one too many times.

"It is rumored that to become a warlock there is a price the person must pay," said Oso. "A terrible price. One that the person doesn't realize until it is too late." Talking about such things made him uncomfortable. He started pacing in front of the bars. He would like nothing more than to escape, but he didn't see how it could be done. There were too many reivers and too many warlocks, and many of his people were too weak. What Thomas wanted to do was admirable, but also impractical.

"It is said that to become a warlock, you must sell your spirit to the Shadow Lord. Only then will that person be given the power he or she so desperately craves. The power to destroy nature."

Thomas had heard much the same story from Rynlin and Rya. Though it had never been confirmed, he accepted it as the truth. The Shadow Lord never gave anything for free. To gain a part of his power, no matter how small, the cost would be high. The people who were willing to pay it never discovered just how high until it was too late. That was their mistake. He had little sympathy for people so greedy for power that they would do anything to attain it.

"That may be the case," said Thomas. "Nevertheless, we can still escape if we're patient."

"And just how do you propose to do that?" asked Oso skeptically.

Thomas had offered him one surprise after another since they had met a few weeks before. This time he glanced at his friend with worry. Had he been hit on the head one too many times? He was sitting there stoically, lying back against the stone wall. He could only imagine the amount of pain Thomas was in, yet his green eyes glowed with mischief, his smile one of confidence and assurance. It drew Oso in.

"Every three or four days a small group of reivers goes out in search of more workers. Correct?"

"Yes," said Oso, waiting impatiently for Thomas' plan to unfold.

"And they always take several warlocks with them. Correct?"

"Yes."

"Yet they have failed to bring back more workers."

"True."

"You said a few days ago that one of the Highlanders had told you that when we were captured, Killeran had led the raiding party himself because he was so desperate for more workers. The production from the mines had dropped by at least half, so he had taken all the warlocks with him except for a handful."

"Yes, but so what?"

Oso was quickly losing confidence. Maybe Killeran had hit him on the head again, but this time a little too hard. That would certainly explain the huge grin on Thomas' face.

"Well, Killeran wasn't very successful on his last raid. He only bagged us. And with the failure of the smaller raiding parties, it stands to reason that he will have to take another large raiding party out soon because his need for workers has increased."

"How do you know that?"

"I don't. I'm just guessing."

Thomas shifted his back against the stone wall, trying once more to find a more comfortable position. He finally gave up.

"Killeran may be the supposed Regent of the Highlands, but there's someone behind him pulling the strings. It's probably the High King, who wants the gold and silver from the mines for his own coffers. Then he can start acting like a real High King, rather than a showpiece. But you and I both know after working in the mines for the last few weeks that Killeran has not been very successful in achieving his goals, or rather the High King's. I'm certain that Rodric, or whoever is behind Killeran, still needs what he can get from the mines, and he's not getting it. So Killeran has to find more workers if he wants to remain regent."

Thomas took a deep breath. His mind had been working at a furious pace, matched by his mouth, and he had forgotten to breathe. He looked over at Oso and saw the realization dawn within him. Oso was putting all the pieces together for himself now.

"So you see," continued Thomas, "it's just a matter of time before Killeran sends out another large raiding party. All we have to do is wait, and when the time comes, we escape and take everyone with us."

"Well, what good is that?" asked Oso. He knew it for a fact now. Killeran had hit him on the head one too many times. Thomas had lost his grip on reality. "Even if he does take all the warlocks with him, we'll still be stuck in these miserable cells."

"Oso, show just a little patience, all right," said Thomas in exasperation.

"That's really an excellent plan, Thomas," said Oso. "Truly, an excellent plan." The sarcasm in his voice was quite obvious, along with his frustration. "But there is one problem with it.

What about the warlocks? They have Dark Magic. We don't. What do we do about that?" Oso was getting irritated.

"You're right, we don't have Dark Magic," said Thomas, his face now serious, even grim. "We have something better."

White light flashed in the darkness and a tiny ball of flame appeared just above Thomas' palm, illuminating the cell. Thomas was using such a small amount of the Talent, he doubted the warlocks would detect it.

Oso danced back in surprise and fear. "You're a war—"

"No, I'm not," said Thomas sharply. "I'm not a warlock. I don't use Dark Magic. I use a different power, one that comes from nature."

Oso stared at his friend in consternation. This was just a little too much for him. Warlock or no, the ball of flame in Thomas' hand scared him to the very depths of his being. For the first time, he was glad for the steel bars separating them, then realized they would do little against the power Thomas could summon. As the shock wore off, the practical side of his nature regained control of his psyche.

"But there is only one other group of people besides warlocks who can—" Oso looked at Thomas in sudden understanding.

Thomas nodded, knowing that his friend had figured it out for himself. "Yes, I am a Sylvan Warrior."

"But the Sylvana are only a myth," shouted Oso, who immediately lowered his voice. He was still rattled. "If not that, at least long dead."

"I don't think you should tell my grandfather that," said Thomas, letting the small ball of flame wink out of existence. "He doesn't like it when people tell him that."

"Your grandfather? So the Sylvana are still—"

"Yes, we still exist. Maybe not in such great numbers as we used to, but we are certainly not a myth."

"Then why haven't you used your power against the warlocks?" Oso had started pacing again. "Why not just blow a way out of this cell for us." He was angry now. If he had been languishing in this cell for weeks for nothing, he'd—

"Believe me, I thought about it. There are what, about a dozen warlocks in the fort?"

Oso nodded that he was correct.

"Well, I think I can take on the dozen, but that still leaves all the reivers."

"Oh." Oso's anger dissipated. "But I thought Sylvan Warriors were all powerful." He was trying to remember what he could of the legends he had heard, the legends that had now come to life.

"Far from it," said Thomas. "We're much too human, in fact. I can defeat the warlocks, but it would take a great deal of my strength, and just like fighting a lengthy battle with a sword, your body needs to rest. After fighting the warlocks, I would be completely useless. Then you'd have to take on the reivers by yourself. How does that sound to you?"

"Not very good at all," said Oso with a smile, embarrassed by his earlier anger.

"But, if we wait until Killeran takes out his raiding party, and there are only a few warlocks left in the fort, our chances are much improved. I can eliminate them, and still have enough of my strength to give us a much better chance of fighting our way free of the Black Hole and taking everyone else with us."

Oso smiled. He liked the way his friend thought. His initial shock at finding out that Thomas was a member of the Sylvana, a group of legendary warriors supposedly just a myth, was something that he normally would have simply laughed at. But he couldn't. Not now. Though he had not known Thomas very long, their circumstances had allowed Oso to learn much about him very quickly. And that demonstration with the ball of fire was enough to convince him, even if it did make him uneasy.

He certainly didn't understand how Thomas did what he did, and he didn't really care to. If Thomas could help him and his people escape from the Black Hole, he'd believe in anything.

"Then we wait," said Oso.

"Yes, we wait," said Thomas. "And we stay alive."

12

FREEDOM OF A SORT

The next day in the mines resembled another session of torture in Killeran's quarters for Thomas. The reivers escorted him and Oso to the mines separately, keeping them out of the chain gang. They were put to work at the very end of a vein, which was the most dangerous part of the tunnel. Their task was to extend the mine as far as they could, knowing that any missed stroke on their part, or bad luck, could bring thousands of tons of rocks crashing down on them.

Killeran even placed two guards at the other end of the vein. It was a ridiculous precaution on his part, since Thomas and Oso were still chained at the neck and legs, in addition to the shackles now attached to their wrists. Not being able to stretch their arms out wide made their task all the more difficult.

The sharp pinpricks of pain that kept Thomas up all night turned into a constant source of irritation and discomfort each time his grimy shirt ran across his upper body. All he could do was grit his teeth and bear it. Thomas stepped back from the stone wall in front of him, laying his pick against his thigh and wiping his tattered sleeve across his forehead.

He smiled despite his pain. Rya would have an absolute fit when she saw what had happened to his clothes. He wouldn't hear the end of it for months. When he was growing up, she had mended the tears that inevitably occurred, always trying to get a few more months of wear out of a shirt or a pair of breeks. This time she'd have no choice but to throw the clothes away. The holes easily outnumbered the remaining bits of cloth.

Oso also lay his pickaxe against his thigh. He knew that Thomas was still tired and weak from yesterday's encounter with Killeran, so he tried to do the work for both of them. The reivers had been waiting all day for an excuse to urge them to work harder, constantly walking down the tunnel, their curses preceding them and their whips cracking in the air to accentuate their words.

"Another fun day, huh?" asked Oso, grinning despite his weariness. His clothes weren't much better than Thomas'.

"Quiet!" shouted one of the reivers.

The other one felt the need to contribute. "Another word from either of you and we'll send you to the block."

That particular reiver, a short man with a barrel chest and little hair atop his scalp, had been using that threat for most of the day. Yet, neither Thomas nor Oso knew exactly what he was talking about. They simply assumed that it was the headsman's block.

Grumbling something incomprehensible under his breath, Oso retrieved his pickaxe and went back to work. Thomas did so as well, wiping his forehead one more time to keep the sweat from running into his eyes. They soon had a steady rhythm going: as one swung his pickaxe into the rock, the other was bringing his around for another strike.

The pounding of the metal against the stone was mesmerizing, as scattered thoughts wandered aimlessly across their minds. For both, most of those thoughts involved Killeran, and what they would do to the rat-faced man when they gained their freedom.

Finally, after another hour of work, which added another foot to the tunnel, it was time to return to the fort. Thomas and Oso waited patiently for one of the reivers to unlock the chains from their necks so they could slowly make their way out into the twilight of another day missed. When they emerged from the darkness, they were greeted by a red sunset just above the mountains. They didn't have time to enjoy it, though. The two reivers pushed them up the path that led back to the fort.

The walk along the curving path was actually enjoyable, though trudging along the rock-strewn ground with leg irons was a bit tricky, especially in the growing darkness. Several times Oso stumbled on a rock, but Thomas was there to keep him from falling. The reivers were not so lucky. As they came around the last bend in the trail leading up to the plateau that held Killeran's fort, the shorter reiver with little hair tripped on a large rock. His friend tried to keep him from stumbling, but it only brought both of them crashing to the ground, with the shorter reiver absorbing most of the fall.

Normally both Thomas and Oso would have laughed as the two tried to regain their feet without knocking themselves down again, but they were too tired. They simply continued on up the trail, ignoring the cries of the guards and forcing the two reivers to run after them. If Killeran saw Oso and Thomas walk through the gates without their guards, the reivers would prob-ably be the next two bodies in the pit.

The Highlanders had returned from the mines just before them and were being herded into their cages as Thomas and Oso walked through the gates of the fort, the deep mud sucking at their boots. With each step, the brown muck reluctantly let go. It was slow-going and treacherous.

The lines to get back into the cages stretched halfway across the yard, as a reiver at the entrance to each cage counted off as a

Highlander passed by, making sure that the same number who had gone to the mines in the morning also returned. As Thomas and Oso passed the first two lines, many of the Highlanders turned to watch them go by.

Several nodded with respect to the two as they passed. Thomas helping Aric in the mines had spread like wildfire among the other Highlanders. Many had been in the cages for months and given up hope of ever escaping. As a result, they had forgotten what it meant to be free. Sadly, these people seemed to have lost their spirit and pride. The story of Thomas' exploits had revived them. There was life in their eyes again, rather than apathy and hopelessness.

Seeing that, the pain of Thomas' burns disappeared. He had been away from his people for almost half his life, yet he never forgot what it meant to be a Highlander: the sense of honor and integrity, the courage and toughness. Killeran may have taken away his and his people's freedom, but he could never take away what it was that made them Highlanders.

They were approaching the third line of workers when Thomas realized that Oso had picked up his pace. This line moved faster than the others. There were only a handful of Highlanders still outside the cage. Turning in the direction of Oso's gaze, he realized that his friend watched a girl standing at the back of the line. Probably only a year or two younger than themselves, she was pretty, even with the dirt and grime covering her short, auburn hair. Thomas understood why Oso couldn't take his eyes from her. Then he saw what had really drawn Oso's notice. Two reivers walked toward the girl. The malicious grins on their faces told Thomas everything he needed to know.

"Trouble," Thomas murmured.

Oso nodded. His eyes were locked on the girl and the two reivers now standing behind her. Their lascivious sneers confirmed their intentions.

"Go ahead," said Thomas. "I'll take care of these two."

"Keep your mouths shut," said the short reiver walking behind Thomas. He still wasn't happy about falling down and blamed the two boys for it rather than his own clumsiness.

The two reivers behind the redheaded girl stepped forward. One put his hand on her shoulder, while the other pushed her out of the line and away from the cage. Confused for a moment, she quickly realized what was going on and tried to back away from her assailants. She was alone, and there was no one to help her. Her fear turned to terror. She wasn't fast enough, though. The guard behind her tripped her with his foot, and the two reivers laughed uproariously as she tumbled in the mud. One of them leaned down and took hold of the chain around the girl's wrists and began dragging her toward the barracks while the other reiver followed in anticipation.

Oso ran forward as best as he could when the girl fell to the ground, hampered by the chains around his ankles. Nevertheless, his anger drove him forward. He refused to allow his people to be treated this way, much less a young girl.

The guards behind him both let out exclamations of surprise at seeing one of their charges escape. The short reiver, who was only a few inches taller than Thomas, leapt forward in pursuit. He unceremoniously fell flat on his back in the mud, having run straight into Thomas' fists. Though he couldn't stretch his arms out wide, Thomas found that swinging both arms at the same time to be quite effective, especially with a length of steel chain attached. The short reiver lay motionless in the mud, his open eyes staring up at the sky, his neck broken.

The taller reiver was a little quicker. He had already moved a few steps in front of Thomas, his dagger drawn. But he was focused on what was going on in front of him, not behind, so he didn't see his friend's demise. Thomas dove forward feet first. He'd never be able to catch the reiver with the chains around his legs. The mud that had hungered so much for his boots was now his best ally, allowing him to slide forward and tackle the reiver from behind. Thomas took the reiver's legs out from under him and the man fell face down in the mud.

Thomas regained his feet in an instant, scrambling forward on his knees, the chain around his hands gathered together to bring down on the back of the man's head. It was wasted effort on his part. The reiver was so intent on the scene before him that he didn't have time to brace himself. Falling on his own dagger, the sharp blade sliced into his gut. The life had already left his eyes when Thomas rolled him over.

Tearing his eyes from the reiver's lifeless gaze, Thomas saw that Oso had gotten there just in time, knocking over the reiver walking behind the girl, a tall, spare man with long brown hair. Having removed one obstacle, Oso jumped over the girl and, like Thomas, gathered the chains around his wrists into his hands.

The reiver dragging the girl away had lost his grip on the chains and was bending over to take hold of her again, unaware of the approaching danger. As he looked up, he was greeted by the steel wrapped around Oso's hands. The tremendous blow sent the reiver flying through the air. Before he could recover and draw his dagger, Oso was on top of him, bringing his fists down again and again on the man's head and upper body.

It took a few seconds for the tall, dazed reiver to realize why he was sitting in the mud. When he finally regained his senses, he climbed back to his feet with his dagger drawn. Oso was still pounding away on the other reiver with his back turned. The tall reiver ran forward, a vicious grin on his face.

Before he could strike, Thomas was there, having slogged through the mud as fast as he could. Thomas launched himself over the girl and onto the back of the reiver. This one, at least, was smart enough to break his fall with his hands, but he couldn't prevent Thomas from slipping his chains around his neck. Shoving the reiver's face in the mud, Thomas rose to his knees and brought them down onto the reiver's back, preventing him from rising. Crossing his arms, Thomas pulled upward with all his strength.

The reiver grasped desperately at the chain crushing his throat. Thomas refused to lessen his hold as the reiver's face slowly turned red, then blue. His actions became more frantic as he tried to throw Thomas off his back. Thomas only pulled tighter across the man's neck until finally the reiver's hands fell forward into the mud, the strength having left his body with his last breath of air. Thomas remained where he was for a full thirty seconds, just to make sure.

Thomas unwrapped the chain from the man's neck, not bothering to look at his blue and swollen face. Rising to his feet, he was pleased to see that Oso was all right. He had eliminated the other reiver and was now comforting the girl, who was still too afraid to move.

Thomas surveyed the courtyard. He was surprised by the almost total silence that met his ears. He and Oso seemed to be surrounded by statues. No one moved, neither the Highlanders nor the reivers. They were all too surprised by what had just happened. In only a few minutes he and Oso had killed four reivers.

Thomas corrected himself. Actually only three reivers, since one of them fell on his own knife, though, he assumed, it was still their fault. Killeran would not be pleased. If Thomas was lucky, he would be going back for another of Killeran's lessons in pain, and Oso would probably join him this time. If not, well, he didn't want to think about that.

Thomas smiled as he looked around. It felt good to finally act, rather than react. Ever since he had been captured, he had been led around on a leash. A sudden surge of pride ran through him.

"I am a Highlander!" he yelled, his words echoing through the tiny valley. "I will be free!"

It was a foolish thing to do, he knew. But it felt so good. He even heard a few cheers coming from the other Highlanders and sensed their pride.

"You always have to make a scene, don't you?" said Oso, a wicked gleam in his eye.

He had coaxed the girl to sit up, though she still clutched his shirt and used his chest as a pillow for her head. It didn't look like she was ever going to release him, and Thomas thought that Oso wouldn't mind if that were the case.

"Sorry, I couldn't resist."

His shout jolted the reivers in the courtyard into motion. More than a dozen ran toward Thomas and Oso with swords drawn. They slowed down to a quick jog when a few lost their balance in the mud. Oso pried the girl's fingers from his chest and stood next to Thomas. If the reivers were as intent on killing them as it appeared, he and Oso didn't stand much of a chance. But they certainly wouldn't go out without a fight.

Oso stepped a few feet to Thomas' left, giving them both a little more room to maneuver. He made sure the girl was behind him. If nothing else, he promised himself that she would survive. Both Thomas and Oso prepared for the coming onslaught, bending their knees slightly and standing on their toes. Neither picked up a sword or dagger from one of the dead reivers. If they didn't have a weapon, it might persuade the reivers not to kill them immediately. They weren't afraid of dying, but they certainly wouldn't mind avoiding it a little longer.

One of the reivers outpaced his friends and charged toward Thomas with his sword poised above his head. Thomas had no doubt as to his intentions. His body tensed as he waited for the man to come just a little closer.

"Stop!"

The shout caught everyone by surprise, especially the reiver running toward Thomas. The other reivers, who were moving more slowly, came to a halt as they recognized the voice that had issued the command.

The single reiver recognized it as well, but was moving too fast to stop as he slid through the mud. Seeing the predicament he was in, Thomas stepped out of the man's way and let him slide past. A few yards later, the reiver lost his balance and fell heavily to the ground. His efforts earned himself several guffaws of laughter from the other reivers, who circled Thomas, Oso and the girl, their swords at the ready.

Killeran stepped around his men, holding his untarnished white cape around one forearm to prevent it from dragging through the mud. His silver breastplate gleamed brightly, having just been polished for the third time that day.

"What's the meaning of this?"

"Please, Lord Killeran," said the girl. "It wasn't their fault." She motioned toward Thomas and Oso. "Your men were trying to—"

Killeran's face grew a hot red. "Silence!"

The girl stepped closer to Oso, now shaking with fear.

"I don't talk to slaves, girl. Remember that. Sergeant!"

Kursool stepped forward, a look of evil on his face.

"Sergeant, put the girl back into the cage and do her no harm."

Kursool walked between Thomas and Oso and grabbed the girl by the arm, pulling her back toward one of the cages. As she was dragged past Oso she took hold of his shirt.

"Thank you," she whispered. Oso nodded in response.

Killeran waited until she was gone before continuing. "The two boys acting like heroes once again." Killeran counted the bodies. "And four of my men dead." Killeran walked around the two slowly, careful not to fall in the mud. "We shall have to remove this streak of defiance from you, and I know just the way to do it."

13

SEARCHING IN VAIN

The two hawks streaked across the sky, flying just above the treetops along the southern edge of the Highlands. Banking around the base of a mountain, they skimmed across a small valley before turning north. It was early evening, the sun no more than a tiny speck in the sky. A strange time for hawks to hunt. They normally searched for prey in the early morning, leaving the night to the owls.

After circling around another mountain and following a small stream farther to the north, the two hawks landed in a small clearing deep within the Highlands. The darkness was almost complete as they settled to the ground near a tiny rivulet of water that ran down from a rocky outcropping. Two bright flashes of white light briefly interrupted the blackness settling over the mountains.

"We'll rest for an hour or so," said Rynlin.

Rya nodded, pulling out some bread and cheese from the small pouch on her belt. Rynlin did the same from his own.

"I thought I sensed him for just a second earlier this afternoon, but I couldn't pinpoint his location."

"So did I," grumbled Rynlin in frustration. "It was for too brief a time, though."

Thomas' grandparents had been looking for him for almost a month. They had waited at first, knowing that Thomas was often gone for a week at a time when he went to the Highlands. But when the faint contact they had with him through their necklaces disappeared, their worry and fear set in. They had found where he had last been before the contact was broken, picking out the signs of the fight that occurred there. Thomas had won the skirmish, but at what cost they didn't know. He wasn't dead. They would have known that immediately. But they couldn't locate him. Some stronger force shielded the power of the necklaces, and that could mean only one thing.

Rynlin settled down next to Rya on a large rock. Rya absently fingered the necklace hanging outside her shirt, tracing the curls of the unicorn's horn. Rynlin sat there in silence. His wife tended to talk to herself when she was worried, and he had learned long before not to interrupt her mumbling.

"That boy will not be wandering through the Highlands by himself ever again," she was saying. "I don't care if I have to take him over my knee. There is no way he will be out of my sight again. He's too young to be out on his own. Much too young."

Soon her rambling became incomprehensible, and Rynlin didn't pay attention anymore. Instead he stared off into space, a grim expression on his face.

After a few minutes, Rya realized what she was doing. She looked over at her husband and saw that he had only taken a few small bites from his cheese. He needed his strength if they were going to continue searching for their grandson. Experienced as they were in the Talent, it still took a great deal of energy to change shape and maintain it for so long a time. She was going to remind him to eat some more, but decided against it.

Rya had seen that black look on her husband's face only a handful of times before, and usually under only the direst of circumstances. She decided against talking to him. His anger and frustration were plain. Though gruff on the exterior, she knew that Rynlin cared for his grandson a great deal. Woe to any person who might try harming Thomas. When it involved a member of Rynlin's family, his wrath knew no bounds.

They sat there in silence for almost an hour, both munching on their cheese and bread but not really tasting it. Finally, Rynlin rose from his seat and walked toward the center of the clearing. Rya brushed the crumbs off her hands and followed.

Twin flashes of bright white light again lit up the clearing. Two large hawks appeared, standing majestically where Rynlin and Rya had been. Without a sound, the birds of prey lifted off into the sky, their powerful wings quickly pulling them higher. They flew with a purpose. Their grandson was alive, for now. They promised themselves that they would find him, and when they did, whoever had taken him from them would regret it for the rest of their very short lives.

14

THE BLOCK

The lash bit into Thomas' flesh, reopening a long cut across his back already encrusted with dried blood. The lash bit again and again and again, but Thomas refused to cry out, gritting his teeth against the sting. Each stroke sizzled against his skin, sending sharp spikes of agony through his body. That, along with the dozens of tiny burns that had not yet healed, made him feel like that's all there was to life. Pain. Pain in which you could hide from the problems of the world, the struggles of your life, and slip away quietly to a calm and peaceful place. Where pain could no longer touch you. Where nothing could touch you.

Thomas shook his head to clear the cobwebs. He was on the verge of unconsciousness again. He should have welcomed it. It eliminated the pain for a time. But there was a danger. He was afraid that sometime soon, he would drift off and never wake up again. His entire body was on fire. There was only one thing in his life right now, and that was the sharp flash of pain that surged through him when the lash struck his back or chest.

Finally, after ten sharp bolts of tingling misery, it stopped and was replaced by the deep burn of his many wounds.

Killeran had told Kursool to make sure Thomas and Oso hurt more than they ever thought possible, but to ensure that they also remained alive. For three days Kursool had succeeded. On the stroke of every hour, Thomas and Oso were dealt five lashes. Every hour on the hour for three days. And they were still alive.

Thomas looked over at his friend. The reivers had started with him first this time. Oso was unconscious now. Thankfully, his friend was still breathing, as his chest rose and fell in a slow rhythm. He envied his friend in a way. It was the only way to escape the pain, if only for a few minutes.

The reivers assigned the task of caring for the two prisoners laughed heartily as they returned to their barracks. It was early morning, with dawn just a few hours away. The biting cold actually refreshed Thomas, easing the pain to a certain extent.

He and Oso were on the block, something that they hadn't paid much attention to during their time in the Black Hole. Situated near the gates of the fort, so anyone entering or leaving would see it, the block functioning as a small stage, and one of the few places in the fort not covered by mud. Kursool had chained Thomas and Oso to it, their wrists attached by long steel lengths to metal shackles set in the wood floor. They could sit or even lie down on the block, but more important, they could be made to stand up, giving their jailers clear targets for their lashes.

15

RESPECT

The sun was about to brighten the sky when the first chain gang of workers made its way slowly out through the gates of the fort on their way to the mines. As they passed by, each one turned to the right to look at the block. Thomas and Oso stood there proudly, refusing to sit or lie down. They would not show any sign of weakness, though their bodies could barely keep them upright. The torture was taking its toll.

Most of the Highlanders stared at the two, their pride obvious. Some nodded in respect. They remembered now what it was like to be a Highlander, what it was like to be free, after such a long period of time in the mines. Killeran had hoped that by placing the two on the block, the gradual deterioration of their spirit would cow the Highlanders into working harder. The opposite had happened. It had made them angry — and proud.

Though their bodies cried out for peace — their torsos covered by cuts, bruises, welts and dried blood — Thomas and Oso ignored the pain as best they could. Their shirts had been reduced to tattered blood-red ribbons, yet they wore them as coats of arms.

Oso stood up a little straighter as the last chain gang of workers exited the fort. The girl they had saved was with them. She had recovered from the attack by the two reivers, the bruises on her wrists having healed. Each morning and evening, she locked eyes with Oso. Everything she wanted to say was in her eyes, and Oso never failed to read them.

Oso had regained consciousness shortly after the reivers returned to their barracks earlier in the morning. Thomas made him drink from the water skins the reivers left for them. The cool liquid revived him somewhat. Yet the only thing that could really help would be weeks of bed rest. At the moment Thomas could think of nothing better than being in his bed back home on the Isle of Mist, but it was a foolish wish, and he banished it from his mind. Killeran approached from across the muddy green with several reivers in tow.

"A wonderful morning, is it not, gentlemen?" Thomas wanted nothing more than to shove Killeran's insolent grin into the mud. "So how are you faring today?"

Killeran knew that neither of the two would respond to his questions, but he still enjoyed taunting the two would-be heroes.

Thomas and Oso stood there in silence, though Thomas watched Killeran with keen eyes. Something was going on. Ever since they had been placed on the block, the whippings had taken place exactly on the hour, every hour. But the reivers had missed the last four. And Killeran had not shown his face for the last few days, staying cooped up in his headquarters with his sergeants.

Thomas took a moment to study the camp. There was more activity going on than usual, with many more reivers out and about at this early hour than Thomas had ever seen before. The reivers were preparing for something. Maybe that's why Killeran had forgotten about them.

"I know you've enjoyed your time in the spotlight, and I

certainly would like to extend it," said Killeran, wiping an imaginary piece of dirt from his silver breastplate. "Unfortunately, other pressing matters prevent it, so we'll be returning you to your cells for the time being. If you're still alive when I return—Well, I don't really expect that to be the case." Killeran laughed at his own joke, as did his men. "Take them down and put them back in their cells."

As the reivers hastened forward to obey Killeran's command, Thomas and Oso looked at one another. Their expressions remained grim, but their eyes danced with pleasure. Killeran was finally leading another raid, and with him would go the warlocks. The exhaustion and pain that had become a common part of their lives dissipated. They felt restored, as if the wounds on their bodies were miraculously healed. Their thoughts immediately turned to escape.

16

ANTICIPATION

"Just as I told you," said Oso. "Killeran's taking them out now. It gives them a better chance of avoiding the Highland scouts."

The moon was well up in the sky, shining down brightly on the earth below. It was close to midnight, and though the reivers tried to leave the compound as quietly as possible, with such a large number of men and horses it was virtually impossible. Why Killeran demanded absolute silence, Thomas didn't know. He was in his own fort. Why should he care if anyone else in the Black Hole knew what was going on?

It only created more confusion as the reivers tried to organize through whispers and hand signals. Thomas had a hard time not laughing at the scene before him. Whoever led the pack horses was not doing a very good job. The leads for the dozen or so animals were hopelessly entangled, and any reiver unfortunate enough to ride by often got caught up with them. Thomas would have laughed, if not for his desire to see Killeran take his troop of soldiers out through the gates as quickly as possible.

"You were right about that," replied Thomas. "I just wish they'd move faster."

About an hour later, a figure in a white cloak followed by more than a dozen cowled figures appeared before the milling mass of reivers, then trotted their horses out through the gate. The reivers followed after him, still trying to find some semblance of order.

Thomas dropped down to the floor, letting go of the two bars of his jail cell he was using to see out through the window. The past day had done wonders for his tortured body. The pain remained, but his spirits rose appreciably. He was even a little excited. Their opportunity for escape was creeping closer and closer.

Thomas counted fourteen warlocks riding out with Killeran, which meant that only two remained within the fort. Killeran was in desperate need of more miners, and either he was extremely confident that he had found a new source of workers, or he had reached the point where he had to take more risks. When he returned to the fort, Thomas was certain that he would view his latest expedition as a mistake.

Oso dropped down to the floor. "The raiding party is on their way." Just like Thomas, the day of rest had proven to be extremely beneficial for Oso. Much of his strength had returned, and he felt rejuvenated.

Thomas nodded. "Then we wait."

He planned to give Killeran time to get several leagues from the fort. As soon as Thomas made use of the Talent, the warlocks with Killeran would know. He wanted to ensure that no matter how long it took them to put their plan into action, the warlocks would not return in time.

17

DECISION

"A good evening to begin a raid, milord," said one of Killeran's sergeants. A tall man, with a wispy mustache.

Killeran was in no mood to talk and ignored the attempt at conversation. It was a good evening to begin a raid, but something nagged him. He felt as if he had forgotten something. For the hundredth time he rethought his decision to leave those two boys alive. A small voice in his mind kept telling him that he had made a mistake by not killing them.

In the beginning, he had been intrigued by the small one with the intense green eyes. He thought he should recognize that one, since he seemed familiar enough. He just couldn't put the pieces together. During the month the two had been in the fort he had tried many times to break them. Still, they remained defiant.

Killeran berated himself mentally. If he could break those two, just think what it would do to the other Highlanders. Production would increase tenfold. Yet they hadn't been broken, and the Highlanders were getting more difficult to deal with because of them. Enough was enough. Those two were having the wrong effect on his workers. When he returned, they would die. Then he could be rid of them once and for all.

18

TASTE OF THE TALENT

Thomas and Oso waited impatiently as the minutes passed. Every so often, Oso climbed the bars to look out through the window and watch the moon move slowly across the sky. He then paced in his small cell, rubbing his hands together in anticipation. Thomas sat quietly against the wall, enjoying the feeling of the cool stone on his back. It would take more than a day for his wounds to heal, but the cold alleviated some of the pain. He spent most of his time trying to relax, though it was difficult with the tiny pinpricks that constantly shot through his body. He wanted to be rested when the time for action came. He would need to concentrate.

As he sat back against the wall, for some strange reason a picture of the girl he saved in the Burren formed in his mind. He hadn't thought about her for quite some time, and he had no idea why he did now. She truly was beautiful, and there was a spirit within her that he found hard to resist. If she was the daughter of the king of Fal Carrach, he was certain that she would be an excellent queen some day. He had seen it in her eyes.

Abruptly, Thomas rose to his feet. "It's time. Killeran is several leagues away."

Oso stopped in his tracks and looked down at the floor sheepishly. He had been pacing back and forth along the same trail for hours. He half expected to see that the stone beneath his feet was worn down a few inches. Distracted, Oso didn't think to ask how Thomas could be so precise with respect to Killeran.

"What do you need me to do?" he asked in anticipation.

"Nothing just yet," replied Thomas, seeing a flash of disappointment on his friend's face. He smiled. His friend was as anxious as he to be gone from this cursed place. "Let me take care of the remaining warlocks first. Then we leave."

Thomas turned around and looked up at the window above him, catching just a glimpse of the stars. Closing his eyes, he delicately took hold of the Talent. A surge of welcome energy immediately consumed him. With the power flowing within him, he felt more alive than he had in a very long time. Thomas took a few moments to relish his closer contact with the power of nature, letting it play across his body and through his heart and spirit.

He then turned his attention to his task. Thomas stretched out his senses carefully, not wishing to alarm the warlocks. He had guessed that only two remained, but he could be wrong. He couldn't afford to make a mistake now. While engrossed in what he was doing, he would be vulnerable to an attack by someone with knowledge of Dark Magic. If that happened, his chances for escape would disintegrate. His only alternative then would be death.

Slowly he reached out, pushing his senses toward the warlocks' barracks. Thomas pulled his senses back quickly. He had been right to be careful. He had miscounted. Three warlocks remained in the fort, all asleep. Luck was smiling down upon him, at least for now. He would have to concentrate all the more because of the additional warlock.

Thomas extended his senses once again, until he was at the very edge of the three warlocks' awareness. Crossing over that obscure line would alert them to his presence and give them time to defend themselves, so he remained where he was and gathered his strength.

With a lightning quick strike he attacked, focusing the full force of his will on theirs. The speed and strength of his assault shattered their magical defenses and destroyed the minds of the three warlocks, who would never wake. It certainly wasn't the bravest way to fight someone, but it was effective. And at the moment, that was all that Thomas cared about. Having eliminated the primary threat, it was time to put the rest of his plan into action.

"It's done," said Thomas as he turned back to his friend. "The warlocks are no longer a problem."

"But how ..." began Oso, before what he saw next dried the words in his mouth.

Thomas had focused on the lock to his cell, laying his hand on it. In a flash of blue light, the lock melted. Thomas pushed the door open and then did the same to Oso's cell door.

Oso had never seen anything like it before. He was both amazed and frightened. Yet, now was not the time to think on it. It was time to act. Oso leaped out of his cell, glad to be free of it, and followed Thomas up the steps that led to the reivers' barracks.

Thomas motioned with his hand for Oso to stop and remain silent as they reached the large steel door at the top of the stairs. It was, of course, bolted from the other side, but Oso didn't worry about that after witnessing what his friend had done to the other locks.

A small part of his mind told Oso that he should fear his friend. The more rational part acknowledged the benefits of

Thomas' newly displayed abilities. He knew how the Shadow Lord created warlocks, imbuing them with Dark Magic. He also knew the stories of those with abilities similar to those of the warlocks, but who applied their skills in the fight against the Shadow Lord.

Thomas again extended his senses and was pleased by what he found. Killeran had taken more of his men with him this time than Thomas had expected. Only a quarter of the reivers remained, and some of those were on guard duty. Three were awake in the barracks, playing cards. Even better, they were in the small room on the other side of the steel door. The rest of the reivers were asleep in the main hall, which was all the way down the corridor. If he and Oso were quiet, they could make it out of the barracks without raising an alarm.

"There are three in the room beyond the door," whispered Thomas, using the door as a canvas to show where they were situated. All three sat with their backs to the door in the far corner of the room. Thomas considered using the Talent on these three as well, but decided against it. It would have made things easier, but he wanted to conserve his strength. He knew that he would need it before the night was over, and the constant work and torture had weakened him. "We eliminate them quietly. I take the one on the left, you take the two on the right." Oso nodded, pleased that it was time for him to play a part. "The rest of the reivers are in the barracks. If we do this right, we get out without any problems, then head for the cages."

Thomas focused on the steel door, contemplating it for a time. He would have to do things a little differently since the lock was on the other side. Extending his senses, Thomas formed a picture of the mechanism in his mind. He then sent a thin stream of energy into it, which melted the bolts within the door soundlessly. Oso had moved up right next to the door while Thomas was at work and kept his hand against it so it wouldn't swing backward and alert the reivers. In a few seconds, Thomas finished and joined Oso on the top step.

"Ready?" he asked.

Oso nodded again. Giving the door a gentle push, they stepped through the opening on silent feet. The reivers never knew what hit them. Thomas and Oso reached their quarry at the same time and took hold of their heads from behind, giving them a quick jerk. The first two reivers were dead before the third even looked up from his cards. Oso moved behind him and broke his neck with a quick jerk as well.

They dragged the three reivers from their chairs and put them on the other side of the steel door, pulling it closed. The bodies on the other side would prevent it from swinging open. If anyone came into the room, all would appear normal. Completing that task, they left the room and went down the hallway that led to the main door.

Oso was about to pull the door open when Thomas' hand on his forearm made him stop. Thomas motioned to an open room off to their left. Oso looked at his friend and smiled. The storeroom, and it was filled from top to bottom with weapons. They trotted into the room marveling at their luck. Oso bent down and dug into a pile of swords, looking for one that would suit him. He almost jumped back in surprise.

"This one is yours," he said, handing Thomas his grandfather's sword.

If Oso recognized the blade as anything more than a plain but finely crafted sword, he didn't show it. After Killeran took it from him, Thomas never expected to see it again. His luck certainly was good tonight. While Oso quietly rummaged through the many remaining blades for one of his own, Thomas searched for something else. After a few minutes, he finally found it — a large leather bag.

He went back to his friend, who was admiring the blade he had just found. It was of excellent quality, with intricate designs carved into the base. Oso grunted in satisfaction after testing the balance and swinging it through the air a few times.

"Fill this up with anything you can — daggers, swords, whatever — while I check outside," said Thomas, thrusting the bag into his friend's hands and making his way to the main door. Oso quickly went about his assignment, trying to stuff as many steel blades into the bag as would fit.

Thomas extended his senses into the courtyard before opening the door. No one was around. It hadn't taken long for the guards who regularly walked along the top of the walls to slack off in Killeran's absence. They had all congregated in one of the watchtowers playing a game of dice. Opening the door quietly, Thomas stepped outside. The moon was beautiful, but it was also a hindrance. He would have preferred a dark, cloudy night rather than one with a full moon.

The entire fort was deathly quiet as Thomas walked a few steps out into the muddy courtyard. The reivers had closed the gates after Killeran left. Thomas assumed that the men on the battlements figured they would have enough warning if they actually were attacked. Well, they had never thought an attack could come from inside the fort. That would work to Thomas' advantage. Off in the distance he saw the five steel cages that housed the Highlanders. It wouldn't be long now before the freedom they craved would be theirs once again.

Oso silently padded up next to Thomas, having filled the bag now hanging over his shoulder to bursting with daggers, swords and maces.

"Ready."

"Good," said Thomas. "On to the next step."

Thomas had laid out his plan for escape earlier in the day. Oso approved. He was fairly certain that he and Thomas could escape from the fort quite easily on their own thanks to Thomas' unique abilities, but he worried over Thomas' refusal to go anywhere without the rest of the Highlanders. Oso also wanted to free as many of his people as he could, but he thought it might be more difficult than Thomas envisioned.

Oso nodded. Hugging the wall of the reivers' barracks, he and Thomas moved stealthily through the night, edging closer to the slave pens.

19

THIEVES IN THE NIGHT

Anara leaned backed wearily against the steel bars of the cage, softly humming a lullaby to the two small children lying in her lap. Their mother had died a month before and the shock had not yet worn off. The children thought that their mother would always be there for them. They were forced to learn the harsh lesson that that was not always the case, especially when you worked in the mines. She really didn't mind taking care of them. Someone had to look out for them, and there were too many children here without parents as it was.

Anara continued to hum, absently stroking their hair, if for nothing else than to occupy her time now that the children slept. Her voice was soft, but her expression harsh. She gazed out through the steel bars with daggers in her eyes. Brushing a strand of dirty auburn hair from her face, she wished for a good steel blade.

Before she was captured she had been very good with a dagger. She imagined throwing it between the bars and striking her target. In this case, the middle of the reiver's chest who stood guard near the cage. She smiled at the thought. He was only a dim shadow in the darkness, but she knew that her aim would be true. Normally there were two, but with Killeran having taken the bulk of his forces on another raid, the skeleton force he left behind was stretched thin.

She laughed softly at her defiance. She had not yet given in to the hopelessness that pervaded the cages. The mines were deadly enough, but they weren't the main reason people died here. Most who died here had given up hope. They no longer cared about living. It had happened to the mother of these children, even though she had something to live for. After surviving in the mines for several months Anara knew that was the first step on the road to death. And she wasn't ready to die just yet. Not after what those two boys had done for her.

When the two reivers approached her she knew immediately what was on their minds, yet she could think of no way to stop them. The other Highlanders couldn't offer her any help, since all the men had already entered the cages. A part of her simply gave up, knowing that what was about to happen was inevitable. Then the two boys, the one with the sharp green eyes and the large one with long blond hair, came to her aid.

She had never seen anything like it before. The ease with which they killed the four reivers shocked her. Afterwards, the tall one stood over her like he was her guardian. She felt safe in his arms, and she had not wanted to let go. There was something about him that stuck with her. She didn't know what it was, an awareness perhaps, but it was as if they belonged together. She soon discarded the idea as a daydream, a trick of the mind to get through the drudgery of working in the mines. Nevertheless, the thought still appealed to her.

One of the girls sleeping in her lap shifted slightly, trying to find a more comfortable position. Gazing down to make sure she was all right, Anara continued to stroke their heads. She had learned after two sleepless nights that it helped to make them feel safe. She had never thought she would become a mother at such a young age, even if not in the traditional sense of the word.

She was about to drift off when out of the corner of her eye she saw a flash of movement. Looking up quickly, she twisted her neck around, trying to find the source. Nothing was there. It must have been her imagination.

Wait a second! The guard! Where was the guard? His familiar, if unwanted, silhouette was gone. Then she smiled for the first time since she had arrived at the Black Hole. Two shadows — one large, one small — ran toward her. It seemed as if her daydream might not have been a daydream after all.

20

BREAKOUT

Thomas and Oso reached the back of the reivers' barracks without incident. It would have made things easier for Thomas if it was darker, but he'd just have to make do with the full moon. The first cage was only a few hundred feet beyond where they were hiding. The sloping roof of the building offered Thomas the darkness he desired. But they could not see the other cages from their current position.

Sneaking up on the guards would be much more difficult than when he freed the Highlanders the first night he had met Oso. The grass in that clearing had been up to his waist, thus helping to conceal his approach. Here, there was nothing but a muddy field. He would have to try a different approach. Thomas motioned for Oso to remain where he was.

"Wait until I signal for you," he whispered.

Thomas rose from his crouch, put his sword back in the scabbard he had fastened to his back, and pulled his dagger from its sheath. Then, as if he was going for a leisurely walk in the moonlight, he strode confidently toward the guard.

Oso was too shocked by Thomas' audacity to stop him. "What the—"

In a blink of the eye, Thomas disappeared. He had been walking just a few feet away from the barracks, and now he was gone! Oso rubbed his eyes, thinking it might be a trick of the moonlight. When he opened them again, all he saw was the cage and the guard standing before it.

What was Thomas doing? Where had he gone? Oso decided that it was best to remain where he was. He had almost jumped out of his skin when Thomas melted the locks in his hands. Why should he be surprised if he could disappear whenever he wanted? Settling back against the stone wall of the building, he placed the bag of weapons on the ground by his feet.

Thomas walked a few paces toward the first cage, the mud sucking hungrily at his boots. Taking hold of the Talent, he pulled the energy within him, molding it to the scene around him. His grandmother had been right. The more you did something, the easier it became. In seconds he became invisible. Now all he had to do was maintain the illusion until he was close enough to the first guard to strike.

He took his time as he silently walked toward the reiver, who focused on the cage before him rather than worrying about someone coming at him from behind. Thomas placed his feet carefully. Even if he maintained the illusion, the sound of him falling in the mud would surely give him away. Though it took only a few minutes to cross the open space, it felt like hours. A clock kept sounding in his head, the tick-tocking punctuated by the words, "Hurry! Hurry!"

As he approached the reiver from behind, Thomas glanced around quickly to make sure no one was watching. Certain that they were alone, Thomas stepped silently behind the guard, who was not much taller than he was. Stretching his hand around the reiver, Thomas clamped his hand over the man's throat as he stabbed him in the back, his dagger puncturing the reiver's heart. The man slipped silently to the ground in Thomas' arms.

He would have preferred to drag the body away, but there was nowhere to hide it. If he and Oso were fast enough, leaving the guards where they fell wouldn't be a problem. Releasing his hold of the Talent, Thomas reappeared where the guard had once stood. He turned around and motioned for Oso to come forward. If everything went as smoothly this evening as it had so far, they would all be leagues away from here with the reivers none the wiser.

21

INSTINCTS RETURNING

As the two shadows ran toward the cage Anara quietly woke the children sleeping on her lap and handed them to the woman sitting next to her. She then woke everyone else in the cage, whispering for them to remain quiet. For those who asked questions, she simply told them to look outside the bars. Thomas and Oso appeared at the door to the cage looking like men who had spent most of their lives sleeping in the gutters, standing there in rags and covered in grime.

The encaged Highlanders had never seen a prettier sight. Just as the women from Oso's village had done when they escaped from the hillock, the women in the cage took charge of the younger children. The men helped those who were injured or too weak stand, a few even lifting into their arms those unable to walk. No one would be left behind.

Anara knew that she had been right to hope for escape. Many of the people she met in the cages had said that escape was impossible, that no one had ever left the Black Hole alive. That never bothered her. She always replied, "Well, there is a first for everything. And I mean to be a part of that first."

Someone was surely looking down on her this night. After

Thomas and Oso — she had learned their names from the other Highlanders — protected her from those reivers, she thought that anything was possible. She wanted to shout for joy, but thought better of it. She would celebrate once she was beyond the walls of this dreadful place and on her way back home.

Thomas immediately stepped up to the door as Oso came to stand next to him, the bag of weapons slung over his shoulder. Taking the steel lock in his hands, he used the Talent to guide the power of nature, melting the lock into a smoking ball of metal. Remarkably, the heat he generated never harmed his hand, though it was hot enough to burn through steel. He didn't quite understand why, but he certainly wasn't about to complain.

Before the door was even halfway open, the Highlanders had already begun to exit from the cage. Thankfully, they did so quietly and in an orderly fashion, recognizing the need for silence. Even better, the reivers had unknowingly aided in their escape, having taken the chains from their wrists and ankles for the night. The women immediately formed into a circle off to the side with the children inside. As the men exited the cage, they nodded their thanks to Thomas and then took the sword, mace or dagger that Oso offered them.

The men then created a circle of their own around the women, providing two defensive shields to ward off any attack. Though these people had been beaten down for years, they were first and foremost warriors, and their instincts died hard. The transformation from slave to fighter took only seconds, and though they were a little rusty and greatly weakened, Thomas saw from the grim expressions on their faces that they would welcome the opportunity to avenge themselves on those who had oppressed them for so long. The last person out of the cage was the girl they had rescued a few days before.

Anara almost leaped through the open door, so anxious she

was to taste freedom. She immediately ran to Oso, who was about to swing the bag back onto his shoulder. Wrapping her arms around his large neck, she hugged him to her with all her strength, silent tears of joy running down her face. Oso stood where he was, the bag of weapons in one hand, his other in a posture of surprise. He had absolutely no idea what to do. He looked to Thomas for help, but his friend shrugged his shoulders. Thomas appeared as perplexed as Oso felt. Not knowing what else to do, Oso hugged her back. That only made her squeeze his neck harder, but it was a pleasurable feeling.

Abruptly, Anara let go and dropped to the ground. Oso wished she would have hugged him just a little bit longer. Giving him a quick smile, she pulled a long dagger from the bag. Thomas stepped next to her.

"Take the group to the northern edge of the fort," he whispered. "We're going to the other cages and we'll send them over to you. Keep everyone together and keep them quiet. As soon as Oso and I get to you with the last group of Highlanders, we'll be on our way."

Anara nodded and immediately walked over to her group of Highlanders, motioning for them to follow. The ragtag group headed to the north, away from the other cages to wait for the others. Anara had absolutely no idea what Thomas had in mind, since there was no gate or sally door in that portion of the wall, but if he and Oso could escape from the reivers' barracks and then free them without setting off an alarm, she'd follow them anywhere.

Besides, few people had ever given her such a grave responsibility before. By singling her out, Thomas had made her the leader of this motley group, and the men understood that. They were soldiers before anything else and would accept that decision, woman or no. Anara felt her pride swell. She would do as Thomas instructed, and do it well. After what he had done for her, she refused to let him down. She wanted to show that he had done the right thing in placing his trust in her.

22

TICK TOCK

O so again waited quietly, this time at the back of the first cage, as Thomas slipped off into the night. After only a few paces, Thomas disappeared once more.

Eliminating the second guard was just as easy as the first, though Thomas moved a little faster this time. After freeing the first group of Highlanders, the urgency of the situation impressed on him the need for speed. This guard was a little smarter than the first. Rather than standing in one place, he walked his station, circling around the front of the cage in a semicircle so he could look behind it from time to time. He even glanced toward the barracks occasionally.

He made one fatal mistake, however. He was predictable. Thomas found a good spot on the guard's route and waited for him. As he came closer, Thomas recognized the man by the long scar that ran down his face and neck. It was one of the reivers from the original raiding party that had captured Thomas. Killing him would be a pleasure.

As the reiver stepped right next to him, unaware of his presence, Thomas stabbed his dagger through the chain links covering the man's armpit. At the same time, he closed his hand over the reiver's mouth to prevent him from screaming. The reiver began to struggle then slumped to the ground, Thomas' blade having pierced his heart.

Oso arrived at the door to the cage at the same time as Thomas. Taking the lock in his hand, Thomas melted it within his palm, relishing the feel of the Talent as it filled him with power. Just as before, the Highlanders exited the cage quietly, the women forming up around the children, the men taking the weapons handed to them by Oso and circling the women.

Thomas knew that only with Highlanders could things such as this run so smoothly. Their military training immediately took over. Though many of the workers were weak and starved, their eyes held the light of freedom. Thomas knew that anyone trying to extinguish it would be in for a very bad time.

Thomas picked out one of the Highlanders, a grizzled man with wispy gray hairs sticking up from his almost completely bald head. "What's your name?"

"Razel," he replied quietly, fingering the hilt of the sword in his hand eagerly.

"My name's Thomas."

"I know." The man smiled. "Everyone knows."

Thomas nodded, not really understanding why that would be. It wasn't important at the moment, though.

"Take this group down to the northern wall of the fort. There's already a group of Highlanders there. Anara's in charge. Oso and I will send the other groups to you, then we make a break for it. Understand?"

The man nodded, then headed off, leading his group off to the north and away from the other cages. So far so good. Now only three more cages to go.

Thomas' plan went smoothly at the next two cages. Thomas eliminated the guards, then unlocked the doors. As Oso handed out the weapons, Thomas picked out one person from each group to lead them down to the northern wall. They had just finished getting everyone out of the last cage, with the Highlanders forming their defensive circles, when torches flared up around the reivers' barracks, followed by shouts of surprise. Their luck had just run out.

23

UNWANTED SURPRISE

Resin didn't like to take chances. That's why he was still alive. Neither very large nor very strong, he had survived in Killeran's army by his wits alone. That and his unique ability to not so much follow orders, as to make sure someone else paid for his mistakes. He was very good at that. In fact, it was also what kept him alive while growing up on the streets of Tinnakilly. Life in The Decaying City was difficult when not of the privileged class, and he was lucky to escape with just a nose that had been broken a half dozen times. Having a permanently bent nose was much better than a knife in your ribs, which was the most frequent way people exited the beggars' section of the capital of Dunmoor.

When he heard that Lord Killeran was recruiting for his army, he jumped at the chance — a peacekeeping force for the Highlands led by Killeran as regent. Though he really didn't enjoy life as a soldier, he liked living in that rat-infested city the King of Dunmoor so grandly referred to as the Eastern Capital of the Kingdoms even less. By tying his fortunes with Killeran's, he thought he could get rich off the wealth hidden away in that inhospitable land.

All the stories said so. As soon as you crossed into the High-lands, digging a few feet beneath the surface would yield a bounty of gold, silver and assorted jewels. Though Killeran had cultivated his reputation quite carefully in certain circles, the seedier side of Tinnakilly knew his true nature, thus the immediate appeal to Resin and many others like him. Besides, this type of thieving sounded much easier than stealing purses or cutting throats for a few coins.

After a few years of prospecting, he could live out his wildest dreams. So he had left five years ago for the Highlands with images of gold and jewels dancing before his eyes. His decision had not worked out as he had hoped. He was still stuck in the same blasted fort after all this time, with no fortune to speak of and no way to leave the Highlands safely.

It was a cruel twist of fate, he thought, as he meandered back to the reivers' barracks. He knew who was getting rich off the Highlands, and it definitely wasn't him. But there was nothing he could do about that, not without getting his throat slit, or worse. He had seen the warlocks at work, and he knew that when it came to the users of Dark Magic, there were worse fates than death.

Resin had been given the early morning watch a few weeks before, but the hours involved — from midnight to dawn — were better used sleeping than standing atop a fortress wall staring out at a forest where nothing moved. With Killeran out of the Black Hole — a name created by one of the first High-land slaves, and a name Resin thought particularly appropriate — he had decided that returning to the barracks early for some gambling was a better way to spend his time.

Some of his friends used the guardroom leading down to the cells beneath the barracks for their late-night card games. If he was quick, he could play the last few hours before sunrise then sleep away the morning. He doubted anyone would notice if he left his post early. And if there was a problem, he could always blame it on someone else.

Gripping his cloak tightly to his neck to ward off the chill, Resin jumped up the steps of the barracks and hurried inside. He rubbed his hands together briskly as he walked down the hallway toward the guardroom, trying to remember how many gold and silver coins he had in his purse. He was feeling lucky tonight. Very lucky. Once he got his hands on a deck of cards or pair of dice, no one could beat him.

That was strange. Where were his friends? Essar, Nimo and Uzzen never missed a game. Tonight was the night, wasn't it? Resin stepped into the room, puzzled by its emptiness. They always played here, yet except for the table set up against the far wall, it was empty. Kursool had been giving them trouble about where they could gamble a few nights before. Maybe his friends had moved the game. But where? Besides Killeran's quarters and the warlocks' barracks, there was nowhere else to play. And only a fool would willingly go to either place.

Resin stood there for a moment, thinking on what to do. Then he noticed the steel door leading down to the jail cells. He smiled. That must be it. It was the perfect place to play. The two prisoners below certainly wouldn't have anything to say about it.

Pulling out a torch from the rack next to the door, he lit it with one of the torches stuck in the wall. Hurrying to the door, Resin looked behind him first to make sure no one saw him, then slipped through the entrance. He was about to pull the door closed when he felt something against his leg. Looking down, he jumped back in terror, banging his head against the doorframe.

Nimo's sightless eyes stared up at him from the top step, his body perched against the wall. He didn't bother to look for the others. He had survived in the army because of his wits, having learned quickly that acting bravely was the easiest way to get yourself killed. He'd let someone else handle it. Running back through the entrance, torch still in hand, he slammed the door behind him. The crash echoed down the hallway. If that didn't wake the entire barracks, his terrified screams soon did.

24

———

DISCOVERED

The shouts coming from the reivers' barracks told Thomas and Oso everything they needed to know. The slain guards had been discovered, and it wouldn't take long for the reivers to find them. Torches were already coming in their direction as the reivers went from cage to cage.

"Oso, take the lead. Make for the north wall. I'll bring up the rear."

Without hesitation Oso ran to the front of the group and got them moving. Some of the smaller children were scared. You could see it in their eyes. They knew the reivers were coming after them. But the women did an excellent job of keeping them calm and under control. Thomas couldn't afford to have a dozen small children running every which way. He'd never be able to bring them all to safety if that happened. The already grim expressions on the faces of the men darkened. They had tasted their freedom, some for the first time in years. They weren't about to give it up again without a fight.

The group moved as quickly as it could, which was really just a fast shuffle, toward the north wall of the fort. It wasn't long before Thomas saw the other Highlanders waiting for them. Good girl, Anara. She, too, had heard the shouts, and was forming the men into a battle line in front of the women and children. Even in their weakened condition, the Highlanders were not to be taken lightly. Thomas was confident that they could hold off the reivers until Killeran returned with his warlocks. But that would negate all he had accomplished so far. He wanted to get as many of these people into the forest as possible.

As he expected, the reivers were expanding their search, having discovered the empty cages. He'd just have to speed things up. A dozen or so torches were already heading in his direction. Stopping on a small slope just before the north wall, Thomas let Oso take the last group of Highlanders down to the others.

The reivers were almost upon him. He could hear their shouts and curses, and the amazement in their voices at finding their slaves gone. Thomas grinned wickedly. They were in for an even nastier surprise. They had not taken the time to wonder how the Highlanders had escaped from their cages without keys.

Turning away from the oncoming reivers, Thomas focused on the stockade wall a hundred feet to the west of where the Highlanders waited to do battle. Time to put the next part of his plan into motion. In an instant he took control of the Talent, letting it course through his body from his toes to his fingertips. The power flowing within him was indescribable. The self-imposed shackles fell away, and Thomas was finally free to use his Talent to the fullest of his ability. He took in more of the power, and then even more, until he held more of the Talent within him than ever before.

He had waited for this moment for a very long time. All of his emotions pushed their way to the edge of his consciousness. Maintaining his concentration, and his hold on the Talent, he let his anger at what Killeran had done to him and his people rise from a simmer to a boil. The pain that bastard had inflicted on him was nothing compared to that of the men, women and children who had died because of Killeran's greed. Thomas used his anger to focus his will, and soon white-hot rage matched the brightness of the power within him.

His weeks of mounting frustration and anger were about to end. Thomas raised his hand toward the stockade wall. A bolt of white light shot from his outstretched palm, the ball of fire growing larger and larger as it sped toward its target. Gouts of flame spread along the wall as the ball of energy tore through the logs. The power of the blast knocked many of the Highlanders and reivers to their knees. In the midst of it all, Thomas stood there with a wolf-like smile, watching as the surge of energy opened a path to freedom, blowing bits of wood and steel into the forest.

As the flames died down, a hole big enough for ten men to walk through standing shoulder to shoulder took shape. The edges of the hole glowed a bright red, the tiny flames rapidly spreading across the wall. In seconds flames laced the entire north wall. Next time Thomas would have to be more careful. He hadn't planned on using so much of the Talent at once, but he couldn't help himself. After so many weeks of being kept in this wretched place, the taste of it was too sweet to resist.

Oso was on his feet immediately, shaking off the force of the blast and helping Anara and Razel march their groups through the hole. The other three groups followed on their heels. The Highlanders knew that they were being pursued, and that knowledge made them move even faster than Thomas, and even they, thought possible. Their aches and weariness melted away, replaced by adrenaline and desire. They had lost their freedom once. They would not lose it again.

Thomas watched the Highlanders stream out through the hole in the stockade, hoping that Oso could lead them all into the forest before the reivers reached them. He spun when he heard the shouts coming from behind him. The reivers had regained their feet and their purpose. They charged toward Thomas, weapons drawn, their bloodcurdling screams preceding them. In their eyes Thomas was a simple kill — one man with a sword against a score. They had assumed that one of their own warlocks was responsible for the fireball and that it had simply missed its target. They didn't know that the source of that power waited before them.

Thomas stood there calmly, waiting patiently. The reivers' cries barely touched the edge of his awareness. He had not released the Talent yet. As a result, he felt as if he were floating above his body, looking down at what was about to happen. It was a surreal experience, but one he still controlled. These were the men who had terrorized his homeland, his kingdom. These were his people! It was his kingdom! The Highlands were his, and he would not relinquish them!

His anger raged within him, pushing, probing, searching for a way out. His people had been murdered, worked to death and raped. They had suffered any number of indignities, and he had not protected them. His anger and shame flared up within him anew, mixing with his hatred for the reivers, and most of all Killeran. But Killeran was not there, was he? He would have to find another outlet, then. One that deserved a taste of what would now be the consequence for anyone who tried to harm his people.

A tall reiver was no more than twenty paces from him, charging forward at a ground-eating pace. A flowing moustache whipped against his face with every pounding step. Thomas looked the man squarely in the eyes. He could see the bloodlust there. The man enjoyed killing. He actually enjoyed it! The idea revolted Thomas and almost made his stomach turn over. Thomas forced the bile in his throat back down. He would not feel any remorse for killing this man or any of the others. It was simply something that had to be done.

Extending his hand toward the reiver, now only ten paces away, Thomas released a bolt of energy the size of his fist, striking the man in the chest. The energy was so potent, it tore a hole right through his body. The flowing moustache stopped bouncing as the man crumpled to ground, his once murderous eyes now leaden. Thomas didn't wait for the other reivers to get so close, shooting bolts of energy from his hand in every direction. The reivers had no opportunity to escape. In less than a minute it was over, as a score of reivers lay dead at Thomas' feet, their chests missing.

Thomas thought that he should feel sickened by what he had done, or at least remorse, but he did not. He was desensitized to his task. He didn't feel any pleasure at killing these men. If he had, he would have worried. His grandfather had warned him about that. No, he didn't feel any pleasure. Rather, he felt consumed by purpose. He would ensure the safety of the Highlanders trying to escape — at any cost.

He started walking backwards, toward the hole in the northern wall, the oppressive heat caressing his back. The flames that spread from the fireball now played along the very top of the stockade and moving inexorably along the east and west walls. If the reivers didn't take action quickly, the fort would burn to the ground by morning. More reivers came toward him now, not having seen what had happened to their comrades. Pulling in more and more of the Talent, Thomas shot another ball of fire from his hand, which blinded many of the reivers with its brightness.

A crashing boom echoed through the small valley as the fireball blasted into Killeran's quarters, turning the cabin into a pillar of flame. Thomas shot another fireball from his hand, and another, and another, striking the reivers' barracks and the warlocks' barracks, and the last crashing into the Block. The flames hungrily consumed the wooden structures, turning night into day. Eerie shadows danced across the sky. Killeran's fort, the symbol of his reign of terror in the Highlands for the past seven years, was quickly becoming a memory.

Smiling at his handiwork, Thomas stepped through the hole in the stockade and trotted toward the welcoming darkness of the forest. Stretching out his senses, he was pleased to find that Oso had already taken the Highlanders a mile into the woods, and there was no sign of pursuit, at least not yet. As soon as the reivers realized that their efforts at saving the fort were useless, they would come after the Highlanders with renewed vengeance.

Thomas reached over his shoulder and pulled his sword from its scabbard as he stepped between the trees. It wouldn't take him very long to catch up to the others. Soon the weariness would return to the Highlanders as their strength waned. The excitement gave them a needed boost, but the desperation and fear would slowly weigh down their steps. Hopefully by then they would be too far away from the reivers for it to be a concern.

Gripping the hilt of the blade in his hand with a welcome familiarity, Thomas relinquished his hold on the Talent. The power surging through his veins gradually dissipated, much like the waves of the ocean being pulled farther from the shore by the low tide. In its place came exhilaration. After all this time, he had fought back. Yet, it was only the beginning.

25

GOOD FEELING

The small fire had died down to a few glowing embers as the moon lazily crossed the sky. Two indistinct shapes lay huddled next to it, their cloaks drawn tight around them because of the cold. They had both considered stoking the fire just a little bit more to get warm, but they would be on their way soon, even though it was several hours till dawn, and they saw little need for it.

"Did you feel it?" asked Rynlin, throwing off his cloak and leaping to his feet.

He faced toward the west, his eyes taking on a faraway expression. Much to his chagrin, he had been sleeping with his ear bent back, but he ignored the pain. After so many weeks of searching, he had found what he was so desperately looking for.

"Yes, I did," said Rya, standing next to her husband. "From the west, in the foothills." She clutched her amulet tightly in her hand. The warmth had finally returned after so many weeks of cold. She could feel her grandson once again. She could feel his anger and his pain.

"Yes, that's where he is," said Rynlin, certain of it as well.

The amulet he wore was also warm. The cloud surrounding their grandson had vanished. "Few are as strong as he."

Rynlin could feel the tremendous amount of power Thomas had taken control of with the Talent. There was no mistaking it. It was time to go.

Rya looked over at her husband, his grin feral. Her smile probably looked much the same. Whoever had taken her grandson had made a big mistake. And now it was time to pay for it.

A flash of white light illuminated the small clearing for a second, followed by another. When the darkness returned, the two were gone. Only two small shadows climbing higher into the night sky could be seen, moving swiftly to the west.

26

TIME TO HUNT

"How is everyone holding up?"

Thomas dug the tip of his sword into the dirt and used it as a cane. The Talent had taken more out of him than he expected, probably in part because of his having worked in the mines for the past month.

"All right," replied Oso. "But they're tired and weak. We can't move much faster than we already are."

"We've got to. The reivers will come after us soon, and they'll have a very good incentive to catch up with us quickly."

"And what's that?" asked Oso, hands on his hips as he caught his breath.

Highlanders were famed for their endurance, but it was clear that their imprisonment had taken its toll. The five groups of Highlanders merged into one once they reached the forest, with Anara in the lead and Oso serving as the rearguard.

Oso had called a halt after two hours of walking, with most of the Highlanders dropping to the ground in exhaustion. Fortunately, a small stream was nearby. Most would have been happy to remain where they were, but they couldn't. In a few minutes they would have to continue their trek on aching feet and muscles. No one complained, though. It was a small price to pay for their freedom.

"Killeran."

"Killeran? Oh, yes, for letting us escape." Oso let out a loud laugh. "Yes, I can guess exactly what he will do when he returns. I wouldn't be surprised if he puts a few of his own men on the Block."

"He probably would at that," agreed Thomas. "Only, he might have a small problem."

"And what's that?" asked Anara, who came to stand next to Oso. Very close to Oso.

Thomas smiled. Anara was making his friend uncomfortable. Then again, though he fidgeted, Oso made no effort to step away from her.

"When he returns later today, he won't have a Block to use."

"Excuse me?"

"Well, when I was leaving, I wanted to give us as much time as possible before the pursuit began." Thomas shrugged his shoulders. "When Killeran returns, he'll find only the smoldering remains of his fort."

Thomas' smile demonstrated that he was very pleased with himself, and more than satisfied with his work.

"You mean you—" Anara's eyes expanded, and she stepped back from Thomas.

"Yes, I burned down the fort."

Thomas' response made Oso laugh even harder. In his mind, he imagined Killeran's expression when he saw that the seat of his power in the Highlands was now nothing more than a burned out wreck.

"But how did you—" The wild look in Anara's eyes worried Thomas. Oso took hold of her hand in an effort to calm her down.

"Does it really matter?" he asked.

Anara shrewdly examined Thomas, having mastered her

initial shock. Because of Thomas she and her people were free. That was something she could never forget, or repay for that matter. How he did it wasn't important; the fact that he did it was.

"No, it doesn't."

"Good. Now that that's settled, let's move on to more important things. The reivers are no more than an hour behind us. We need to get moving again."

"They couldn't have followed so quickly," protested Anara. "How could you know?"

"Do you really want to know?" Thomas asked.

"Anara, if Thomas says the reivers are an hour behind us, they're an hour behind us," said Oso.

"We need to get these people to a safe place. I know they'll fight, but they won't last very long. And I'm not going to let them die after just setting them free."

The vehemence of Thomas' voice surprised Oso. He had never seen his friend so intense before.

"My home is about a day's travel from here, in the higher passes," said Anara. "It's called Raven's Peak. It's the closest village I know of where we could defend ourselves against the reivers."

A day's trip. It would be a long and hard journey for everyone involved, but they really didn't have any other options.

"Anara, let's get these people walking again. You take the lead. Raven's Peak it is. Oso and I will do what we can to slow the reivers down."

Anara nodded. "Don't you want any help?"

Thomas looked around him. The men were all fighters, as were the women, but in their condition they would be more of a hindrance than a help.

"No, Oso and I will be able to take care of it ourselves. We'll buy you as much time as we can."

Without another word, Anara ran toward Razel, who was sitting with the other leaders Thomas had selected from the five different cages. It didn't take her long to relate what Thomas had said about the pursuing reivers and the plan that they had developed. The men dispersed quickly, and in a matter of minutes, the Highlanders were back on their feet and traveling to the northeast.

"Oso, do you happen to have any bows and quivers of arrows in that bag of weapons you're carrying?"

"Let me see." Oso hunched over the bag and rummaged through it. "You're in luck," he said, pulling two bows and several quivers of arrows from its depths.

"Then it's time to hunt."

"Finally," said Oso. "I've been wanting to do that for almost a month now."

The two men walked back down the trail, the quivers strapped to their hips and the bows resting on their shoulders. The sun was just beginning to peek out from behind the mountains to the east, the hazy red glow pushing back the dark of the night. A day's travel. The Highlanders still had a long way to go, but Thomas was confident that he and Oso could get them there safely.

27

A DANGEROUS ANIMAL

"Anara seems quite taken with you," whispered Thomas as he adjusted the leather guard he wore on his right wrist. Killeran had taken away all their weapons when they were captured, and the reivers had even found the knives hidden in Thomas' boots. But they had never forced him to remove the wrist guard, for which Thomas was thankful. Otherwise, he would have been dead weeks before. Killeran would have recognized the birthmark on his wrist in an instant.

Every so often Thomas extended his senses to get a fix on their pursuers. The reivers were coming after them fast, following the same trail the Highlanders used, but thankfully because of the terrain they would have to come on foot. Their horses would slow them down on this rocky path. When the reivers were no more than ten minutes behind them, he and Oso had slipped into the trees alongside the path.

"What do you mean?" Oso looked at his friend with a quizzical expression.

Thomas laughed softly. "What do I mean? What do I mean? You know exactly what I mean. I saw you when I caught up with the group. She was walking so close to you, from a distance I couldn't tell you two apart."

"That was nothing," protested Oso.

"And what about when we were talking. When she joined us she went right to your side."

"You probably scared her," said Oso, trying to regain some of the ground he was rapidly losing in the conversation. "Those eyes of yours, when you're angry, even scare me sometimes. You're not a very big person, Thomas, but you certainly do know how to frighten people."

Thomas smiled. It wasn't easy to keep Oso on the retreat, even verbally.

"Just what are you saying, Oso?"

"Well, Thomas, to be completely honest, you can be a bit scary. Green eyes glowing, balls of fire bursting forth from your hand. Frightening indeed."

They both laughed softly.

"Well, she does like you," said Thomas. "And I have a feeling that Anara is the type of person who, when she finds something she likes, goes after it. And she doesn't stop until she gets it."

"I know," replied Oso. "That's what worries me."

He was going to say more when Thomas raised a finger to his lips. The reivers had almost reached them. Giving his friend a pat on the shoulder, Thomas moved off to the left, gliding silently between the trees.

In a few minutes, the sounds of footsteps crunching on the loose rock of the path traveled up the slope. Oso marveled at Thomas' abilities. If he could do what Thomas could, he'd bring home a feast to feed a village every time he hunted, rather than a single buck or boar. Then again, it was probably a good thing. How would he carry it all back by himself?

Oso quickly pushed his idle wonderings from his mind. He had work to do. The black-clad reivers trotted up the trail, unaware of what lay before them. Whoever led the reivers in

Killeran's absence was being cautious, sending the scouts out first. Seven in all. The rest of the reivers must be farther down the trail, probably about a half-hour behind this group.

Oso nocked an arrow to his bow and pulled the string back to his cheek. He waited until they were almost even with him before releasing. When Oso heard the twang of Thomas' bow off to his right, he also released. Thomas had moved farther down the trail, so he shot at the back of the group while Oso targeted the front. That way they wouldn't aim for the same target.

He didn't wait to see if his first arrow struck home. The screams of surprise and fear coming from the reivers confirmed the quality of his aim. Oso quickly pulled another arrow from where he had pushed a half dozen into the earth point first. He sighted and released, and then again.

He was about to let another arrow fly, but silence greeted his ears. Looking out through the underbrush, Oso saw the seven reivers lying dead in the dirt and rocks. This would certainly give the reivers coming behind the scouts something to think about, and perhaps even make them more cautious. The more time they could buy for his people the better. Thomas stepped from behind a tree, his bow in hand.

"Good shooting, Oso."

"Thank you."

"Are you ready for the next ambush?"

"More than ready."

"Good," said Thomas. "Let's get going. We'll give the reivers a chance to feel safe again before we dissuade them of that notion."

After retrieving their arrows, Thomas loped off into the forest, moving away from the path. To Oso, he looked more like an animal than a man with his graceful and strong movements. A very dangerous animal.

28

A BRIEF RESPITE

The ambush earned the Highlanders several hours' respite, but that still wasn't enough time. The same short sergeant with whom Thomas and Oso were so familiar led the reivers now. Kursool had become the living embodiment of Thomas' hate, since he was the one responsible for carrying out Killeran's orders. In Thomas' opinion, Kursool enjoyed carrying out those orders far too much, particularly with respect to the Block. Yet it was probably his zealousness that won him a place at Killeran's side. The lines of age and scars of battles past fit perfectly with the short but broad-shouldered man's personality — sharp and abrasive.

Kursool was perpetually angry, and he found his happiness by taking that anger out on others. For the past few weeks, Thomas and Oso had been his targets. At the moment, though, Thomas thought the sergeant's primary motivation might not be anger so much as fear. Kursool had been in charge of the fort when the Highlanders escaped. As a result, he would be the first one to taste Killeran's wrath.

Thomas knew that though the first ambush was a success, much of the day still remained. The sun, which offered little warmth on this cold morning, had not yet reached its midpoint. There was little he and Oso could do against such a large body of men. Kursool had almost two hundred reivers at his disposal.

However, despite the overwhelming odds, because of the first ambush Kursool played right into their hands. Not knowing how many Highlanders were responsible for the attack, he had decided on a cautious strategy. He sent out overlapping five-man squads to scout a quarter to a half mile in front and behind his main force of reivers. By doing so, he hoped to deter more ambushes, and perhaps even flush out the attackers.

Yet, there was one problem. That strategy, though militarily sound, was of little use under the current circumstances. Though the main force had better protection, it left each five-man squad more vulnerable to attack, allowing Thomas and Oso to continue their ambushes and not only buy time for the Highlanders' escape, but also diminish Kursool's remaining forces. Oso had said that some of the larger villages deep within the Highlands were home to several hundred Marchers. He hoped Raven's Peak was one of them.

"There is a group of five coming from the east," said Thomas, materializing out of the forest right in front of Oso. They had picked a spot along the trail where the forest grew thick on both sides. Getting through it required the use of a sharp axe, so they assumed the reivers would stay to the trail. Two hours had passed since the first ambush. With any luck, the reivers had grown lazy since then.

"Would you please stop doing that," grumbled Oso.

He had almost jumped out of his skin when Thomas appeared. One moment he's standing next to a tree, watching for any movement in front of him, the next Thomas is speaking to him from only a few feet away without having made a sound during his approach. It just wasn't natural for someone to move so quietly in the forest.

"Sorry," said Thomas, who found a spot a few trees over where he would have a clear line of sight to the road. "I'll shoot from left to right."

"Sounds good," said Oso.

They soon heard the crunching of boots along the trail. Five black-clad soldiers walked into view across the rocky ground, crossbows held at the ready. In the first ambush, the reivers held only swords and daggers. Thomas and Oso would have to be more careful now. If they missed, these reivers would shoot back.

Thomas waited until all five were in plain sight before firing, Oso having released just before he did. His first arrow took the last reiver in the chest. The man just in front of him heard the loud thunk of the bolt striking home, but before he could turn around and discover what happened, Thomas' second arrow pierced his heart. Both died before their bodies hit the ground.

Leaving the first two to Oso, Thomas pulled a third arrow from the ground, nocked it and aimed for the reiver walking in the middle of the column. The man had seen his two companions in front of him crumple to the ground and was about to flee when Thomas' arrow plunged deep within his chest. In a futile effort, the reiver pressed the trigger of his crossbow, but the bolt flew harmlessly up into the sky as the man collapsed.

"Good shooting, Oso," said Thomas.

"Thanks."

Thomas trotted through the woods and out onto the trail. Dagger drawn, he checked to make sure each reiver was dead before pulling the arrows free. Four came out clean, but the fifth was wedged tight beneath one of the reiver's ribs. During his struggle to remove it, the steel tip broke off. Thomas threw the useless shaft into the forest before rejoining Oso. They had only so many arrows to use and their supplies were dwindling quickly.

"Let's move a little farther down the trail, but not too far. I doubt Kursool will expect another attack so soon after this one."

"A good plan," agreed Oso, taking the two arrows Thomas handed to him and wiping the tips clean on the grass before putting them back in the quiver on his hip.

Oso made the calculations in his mind. Another few hours won, but still a half day or more left. Their work was far from over.

29

FEAR AND WORRY

"Clean through the heart, sergeant," said the reiver as he turned the body over. He looked at the five dead reivers with distaste. He was a veteran of many battles, but he didn't like being around dead men anymore than the next person. "All of them. Clean through the heart."

Kursool studied the five bodies one more time. All dead. All from an arrow straight through the heart. Just like the other five. And the other five. And the seven before that. He had never seen such efficient ambushes before. For the first time in many years he was afraid. He had known those two boys were trouble the minute he had seen them, but rather than killing them right away like he had suggested, Killeran had decided to play with them first.

Well, now the boys were having their fun, along with however many Highlanders were fit enough to join in. Judging by these two attacks, they probably had a dozen or so men with them. It was the only way to explain the ease with which they had eliminated so many of his men.

Unfortunately, a part of his mind — the part he listened to during a battle, the part that had saved his life more times than he could count — told him that he was wrong. A dozen Marchers weren't ambushing his men. It was two, and boys at that. He could see that some of his men already had come to the same conclusion. He could also read from their expressions that they were wondering something else.

In the last hour the reivers had entered territory regularly patrolled by bands of Marchers. If only two boys could do this, what would happen if they came across a squad of Marchers? None of his men had ever seen what those Highland bastards could do when the warlocks weren't around to interfere. Ordering Marchers around while they were in chains was one thing. Matching steel with an angry Highlander was something else entirely. The thought of walking into a group of Marchers terrified him. But what could he do?

He was probably already a dead man for letting Killeran's fort burn to the ground, and the only chance he had for staying alive was bringing the Highlanders back, along with those two boys. If they didn't catch the escaped Highlanders before the day was out, they probably wouldn't catch them at all. Then he and his men would be the hunted, rather than the other way around.

"What should we do, sergeant?" asked another reiver.

Kursool looked at the man with steely eyes. Resin. He had discovered the men murdered in the barracks. Kursool had not bothered to ask him why he had left his post. Time for that later.

"We keep going, Resin."

"But sergeant—"

The man's words caught in his throat as Kursool fixed him with a murderous glare.

"Resin, are you challenging my authority?"

Resin gulped at the implication, his face turning white. The only way to move up within the reivers' ranks was through a duel. Obviously Kursool was one of the best fighters among all the reivers, otherwise he never would have achieved his current standing. Resin was there to make money, and both he and Kursool knew it.

"No, sergeant. Forget I said anything."

Kursool stared at the man a few moments longer. His right hand twitched, hovering over the hilt of his sword. It was too bad Resin had backed down. Killing him in a duel would make leading his men much easier.

"Vanin," he called out.

A tall reiver approached. His long, curly red hair formed a ring around his head that stuck out from underneath his helmet. His overall appearance was humorous, but no one dared to laugh. Next to Kursool, Vanin was the most dangerous man with a blade in the Black Hole, or rather what had once been the Black Hole.

"Yes, sergeant?"

"Take fifty men and increase the size of the scouting parties. I don't want any more surprises."

"Yes, sergeant."

"What was the last report regarding the Highlanders?"

"One of the scouts guessed that they were only a few hours ahead of us," replied Vanin, shuffling his feet uneasily. Vanin was a man of few words and didn't like to talk.

"Good," said Kursool. "Then we can still catch them before the sun sets. Get going, Vanin. We don't have time to waste."

"Yes, sergeant."

Vanin immediately called for the first fifty men in the long column to follow him farther down the trail.

"Let's move out," yelled Kursool as he trotted up the rocky slope.

Kursool's men followed after him, swords drawn and crossbows at the ready. As each man walked past the five dead reivers, their eyes immediately went to the trees around them, scanning the foliage for any sign of movement. They were supposed to be the hunters, they kept telling themselves, not the hunted.

They had gone no more than a mile before the next attack. Kursool was caught completely off guard, not expecting such a bold move from the Highlanders. Somehow the Marchers had slipped behind his scouts. As the first few arrows sped through the air, the reivers stood on the trail too shocked by their attackers' audacity to do anything. Who would risk assaulting such a large group of soldiers?

A larger group of soldiers, most likely. Their shock quickly changed to fear that a Marcher war party surrounded them. The reivers bolted for the trees along the trail, trying to hide behind the thick trunks before they joined their friends lying dead on the rocky path. The once organized column of soldiers deteriorated into a mass of terrified men, knocking one another out of the way as they gave into man's strongest instinct — survival.

Though the attack seemed to last forever, it was over in less than a minute. Kursool peeked out from behind the tree he used for cover. The sight horrified him. More than a score of his men lay dead or wounded on the path, the shafts of long Highland arrows sticking up from their chests.

They had to be facing at least a dozen men. They had to! Two boys could not do so much damage. Two boys could not be so deadly! Kursool tried to convince himself of that fact, but the voice in his head kept telling him that he was wrong. He and his men were up against two boys, and the boys were winning. Shaking off his growing fear, Kursool walked out from behind the tree.

"Back on the trail!" he screamed, hoping that his men didn't smell the fear growing within him. This was supposed to be a simple task because of the Highlanders' weakened condition. He certainly had not counted on this. "Islan! Rumal! Allers!" Three reivers ran forward. "Take ten men each and comb the woods around us. Find the Highlanders who just attacked us, and if you can't find them, find out which way they went."

"Yes, sergeant," they replied in unison, then ran off to gather their men.

Kursool walked over to the men lying in the middle of the path. Two of the reivers had gotten there before him, and both shook their heads with regret. Twenty more men dead or soon to be. Blast!

A shout rang out, and Kursool dived to the ground, as did the bulk of his men. Looking up, he saw Resin standing off to the side with his crossbow. The bolt was missing from his weapon, and a large squirrel sitting on a tree branch chattered down at him furiously.

Kursool pulled himself off the ground. "What are you doing, Resin?"

"I thought I saw something move, sergeant, so I—"

"So you shot at a squirrel," finished Kursool, the contempt in his voice obvious.

"Well, I didn't know it was a squirrel until after I shot at it."

Several of the men around Resin chuckled softly. Kursool turned away from Resin, cursing loudly.

"Leave them where they are," he called to his men. "We keep moving."

He began the long climb up the rocky slope, this time with his sword in hand and his eyes combing the forest around him. His men followed suit. His soldiers were shooting at shadows now. Wonderful. He'd lost more than three dozen men in only a few hours, and he hadn't even seen his enemy. He wanted to turn around and leave this place. Leave the Highlands all together. But he couldn't. He had to keep going. If he didn't find the Highlanders and those two boys, he would never escape the Highlands. Killeran would see to that.

30

A BRILLIANT IDEA

"It's not working as we'd hoped," said Oso between breaths. He and Thomas ran through the forest, having just met one of Kursool's newly strengthened scouting parties. They had come out of it unscathed, and eliminated another half dozen reivers, but they were running dangerously low on arrows. "Kursool is pushing his men hard."

"He doesn't have a choice," replied Thomas. "If he doesn't catch us, he's as good as dead."

"A good reason to keep after us, then," agreed Oso. They had put several miles between themselves and the scouting party, and Oso doubted the reivers they had just attacked would dare to come after them without further assistance. Yet Thomas kept running, and at a very fast pace. If he didn't stop soon, Oso would drop from exhaustion. "Thomas, can we rest for a minute?"

"What? Oh, yes. Sorry about that, Oso."

Thomas stopped and walked over to a fallen tree, using the trunk as a seat. Oso joined him, huffing and puffing as he tried to regain his breath. They sat there in silence for several minutes. Thomas was deep in thought and Oso was too tired to speak anyway. Finally, after the searing pain in his side became a dull ache, Oso turned toward his friend, who had a faraway look on his face.

"Thomas?"

Thomas gave a start, and the misty look in his eyes disappeared. "Sorry about that, Oso. I was just looking around."

"What did you see?"

Oso had quickly grown accustomed to Thomas' abilities, finding his skill at surveying the surrounding forest particularly useful.

"That scouting party we ran into hightailed it back to Kursool. He's still coming after us, but he's going at a slower pace. Unfortunately, Anara isn't moving as fast as I had hoped. She's no more than two hours in front of us, and we've still got most of the afternoon left. We've got to give them more time, but we're almost out of arrows."

"Can you do what you did back at the fort?"

The sight of the fireball leaping from Thomas' hand and blowing a huge hole in the wall of the stockade was seared into his memory. It was one of the most frightening things he had ever seen, but also one of the most pleasurable.

"I probably could," replied Thomas, mulling the idea over in his mind. "But then I'd be useless, no strength left, and we'd still be too far from the safety of that village."

Oso sighed in disappointment. He had forgotten what Thomas had explained to him earlier about the Talent. It was the simplest solution to their problem, but rarely did such things work out as you hoped.

"What about your friends?"

"The Sylvan Warriors?" asked Thomas.

Oso nodded.

"I have no doubt that at least two are on the way. The others —" Thomas let his voice trail off. "The others are so widely dispersed, I doubt any who decided to come to our aid would get to us in time."

Events were going from bad to worse. They had inflicted a huge number of casualties on their enemy, yet Kursool still followed seemingly undeterred by his losses, and now neither he nor Thomas had more than a handful of arrows remaining. Worst of all, Anara required more time than they had been able to provide in order to reach a safe haven. That stuck in his craw more than anything else. He didn't want to let her down. Was Thomas right? Did he like that strong-willed, somewhat possessive redhead? He didn't even want to think about it.

"Oso, I think I've got an idea."

"What?"

"We'll let gravity do the job for us."

"What do you mean by that?" asked Oso, not understanding where Thomas was leading. How could gravity help them?

"Yes, gravity. Come on. I found what we'll need when I was looking around."

Thomas jumped off the tree trunk and trotted into the woods on a course that would take them back to the trail. Reluctantly, Oso followed after him. A few minutes later they reached a point where the trail sloped upwards at a steep angle for almost a quarter mile before settling back down to a relatively easy ascent. Thomas stopped at the base of the steep incline and smiled.

"Yes, this will do nicely."

"What will do nicely?" asked Oso, breathing heavily once again. He was exhausted. Completely and utterly exhausted.

"I should have explained sooner. Actually, I should have thought of it sooner."

"Thomas, slow down for a second, all right. You're talking so fast I can't keep up with you. Now, just exactly what are you talking about?"

"Follow me and I'll show you."

He trotted up the hill, the steep angle failing to slow him down.

Letting out a curse, Oso started after his friend. Every step sent a sharp arrow of pain into his legs. His muscles were ready to give out on him, but he pushed himself forward. Thomas had to be bothered by the exertion of the previous day, particularly after what he had done with the Talent. He was human, after all. But if his friend could keep going despite all that, so could he. Ignoring the aches and pains in his legs, and the cramp that returned to his right side, Oso ran up the last few feet of the slope.

"This is what I was talking about," said Thomas, pointing with his hand back down the path they had just climbed. "We'll let gravity do the job for us."

"Thomas, could you do me a favor and explain just a little bit more?"

Oso found it hard to keep the irritation from his voice. After everything he had been through, he was not in a very good mood.

"Sorry," said Thomas. "It's simple, really. The arrows have bought us some time, but not enough. We need something that can buy us a few more hours. If we can do that, then Anara and the others will make it to Raven's Peak."

Thomas spun and pointed behind Oso.

Turning around, the large Highlander grinned, then laughed. He realized what his friend had in mind. About three hundred feet away, the path continued to meander higher into the mountains, but he and Thomas stood on a relatively flat plain, albeit a small one.

The cliff in front of them was barren of trees, but dotted with boulders and smaller rocks, many of which had congregated on the other side of the plateau. All he and Thomas had to do was move them into position, then let gravity do their work for them. It was a brilliant idea, and Oso couldn't help but laugh at the simplicity of it.

"How did you ever come up with an idea like this?" he asked. "It's perfect."

"I've got some experience with this," said Thomas, who was already walking over to the rock pile. "But then I was at the bottom of the slope, rather than above it."

Oso stared at his friend's back. Thomas was one surprise after another. He'd have to ask him a few more questions about that, but it would have to wait until later. It was time to help Anara and the others. He refused to let his people, and her, down.

31

WARNING UNHEEDED

Kursool and his men had made up a good amount of ground in the past two hours. He still might catch his quarry. Considering the condition of some of the women and children, they could be no more than an hour ahead. But he was worried. It had been more than an hour since the last attack by the Marchers. It had to be Marchers, he kept telling himself. It couldn't be just two boys!

When his four lead scouts came running back with their tails between their legs and blathering about an ambush by dozens of Marchers, he had almost wished for it to be true. At least then he'd know what he was facing. But when they reached the latest ambush site, and saw his men punctured by arrows through the hearts, Kursool knew his scouts were lying. If it really had been a squad of Marchers, those four scouts would not have survived. That's what the part of his mind he didn't want to listen to told him. After the last two attacks, he had pulled his scouts back into the main body of his troops.

Kursool could hear the rumblings of discontent from his men now. Their fear was beginning to take control of their thoughts and actions, which was the first step to disaster for a soldier. At least his men were on their toes. After seeing what had happened to so many of their friends, they had no wish to join them. And they knew they were in much the same situation as Kursool himself. Killeran's anger often had a wide range of outlets. Though they probably would not bear the brunt of it, they would not be immune to his rage.

The path they followed steadily grew steeper, which Kursool actually saw as a good thing. It would slow the Highlanders down even more and give his men more time to catch up. But something was wrong. He could feel it in his bones. Though they were out in the open, the rocky terrain to either side did not lend itself to an ambush. Still, something was not right. The voice in the back of his head was screaming at him now.

Glancing up the steep incline, everything seemed normal. His men had begun the climb up and were making good time. They at least realized the urgency of their situation. Wait. What was that up at the top of the slope? A flash of metal? Perhaps, but he couldn't tell from where he stood. The alarm going off in his brain increased in intensity. Something was wrong. Terribly wrong! But what?

When the ground began to rumble and shake, he finally figured it out. Unfortunately, it was too late for him to do anything but run.

32

A LITTLE PUSH

"Now?" asked Oso.

He was knelt behind a huge boulder they had rolled across the plateau and placed at the edge of the cliff face. They hadn't moved it any closer for fear it would be spotted from below. To the side of the boulder were a few more, though none as large as this one. Oso had inserted beneath it a large tree branch as a crude lever. It had taken them almost an hour to move it because of its awesome weight, but it would be perfect for its task. In front of it were several dozen smaller rocks of various sizes.

"Wait just a moment longer," replied Thomas. He was at the very edge of the cliff, using some of the boulders to hide himself from Kursool and the reivers. "They've just started their ascent. I want them farther up so they can't escape."

Oso grinned. Thomas had a mean streak in him. Oso liked that. He readjusted the lever slightly, trying to dig it deeper beneath the boulder.

Thomas scrambled back from his position on the slope. "Let's do it. They're right where we want them."

He and Oso both took hold of the lever and pushed down

with all their might. The trunk of the small tree bent slightly under the pressure, but the boulder refused to budge. They redoubled their efforts, but still no luck. They were losing time. The reivers would be up the slope in only a few minutes. If they didn't get the rock moving, they'd have no chance to escape.

They tried again, throwing everything they had into it. Thomas draped himself on top of the lever, trying to use his body weight to nudge the boulder forward. Still it refused to move. He couldn't believe it. After everything they had gone through. Even Oso, with his massive strength, couldn't budge the huge rock.

Opening himself to the Talent, Thomas realized just how weak he was as a wave of exhaustion ran through him. What he had done at the fort had taken more out of him than he thought. He was at the very limit of his strength.

Delicately taking hold of the power surging within him, Thomas fashioned a large lever in his mind and inserted it beneath the boulder. Ever so slowly, he exerted pressure on it. Finally, the huge rock began to move, inching forward slightly before settling down once again. The reivers were almost to the top of the cliff. Thomas and Oso had to hurry. The boulder had to move now!

Oso's face turned a dark red, the veins in his neck straining to the point of bursting. His eyes were closed in desperation as he tried to will the rock down the slope. It had inched forward before, then returned to its original position. He too knew that if it didn't budge, their efforts would be wasted. Kursool would have no trouble catching the Highlanders once he had gotten past them. Oso pushed down on the lever with all his might. The trunk of the tree cracked ominously as it resisted the two forces being applied to it.

Gathering his will a final time, Thomas poured as much of his energy as he safely could into the lever he had created with the Talent. He was losing his strength rapidly, but he refused to stop. The boulder had to move. It had to! The reivers were almost to the top.

Finally, after what seemed like an eternity, the huge rock inched forward slowly, then inched forward some more. Thomas gave the boulder a final nudge with the Talent. After teetering on the edge for what seemed like an eternity, the boulder started rolling slowly down the hill, the smaller rocks tumbling down before it. The screams that traveled up the cliff face told Thomas and Oso all they needed to know.

They moved to the other boulders they had lined up next to the larger one. It was much easier to get these moving because of their reduced bulk. Soon four more large boulders followed the first down the slope to crash into whatever stood in front of them. Not bothering to look at the result of their handiwork, Thomas and Oso trotted across the plateau and began the arduous climb up the trail. Both were exhausted from their efforts, yet they pushed themselves onward.

The weakness that Thomas thought he had conquered after he had destroyed the fort had returned. His muscles didn't want to obey him anymore. He didn't blame them a bit after everything they'd been through. Thomas and Oso had done everything they could to slow down Kursool and his men. Now their only hope was reaching Raven's Peak before the reivers.

33

UNSTOPPABLE FORCE

As the huge boulder balanced on the edge of the incline before beginning its rapid descent to the bottom, Kursool stared in horror at the scene unfolding before him. The screams of his men trying to escape the onslaught washed over him, yet there was nothing he could do but run back the way he had come until he reached the relative safety of the trees.

His men fled in all directions, doing whatever they could to get out of the way of the huge stones bearing down on them. The smaller rocks were dangerous enough. Though no larger than a man's fist, one of those rocks would easily crush a man's skull or chest.

The men who had almost reached the top of the slope fared the worst. They had nowhere to go but down, and their frenzied efforts to do so were no match for the speed of the boulders. The smaller rocks knocked dozens of his men to the ground, and those who were lucky enough to rise were crushed by the huge boulder that followed in their wake.

The boulder swept the trail clean of his men as it hurtled down the slope and crashed into the trees below, finally coming to a stop after plowing several dozen feet into the forest.

Kursool sighed with relief. It could have been much, much worse. But why was the ground still shaking?

Looking back up the slope, his worst fears were confirmed. A smaller boulder had begun its descent, followed by another, and yet another, each one knocking dozens of smaller rocks before it. The men who remained on the slope were doomed as the stones pounded over them. Those who had stepped from their cover dived back, often not in time to escape. Kursool himself dodged behind the tree he used as a shield as several smaller rocks hurtled past him. Cries of agony echoed around him as he hunched down in fear.

34

HELP ARRIVES

"How much farther do we have to go?" asked Thomas.

He and Oso had caught up with Anara and the Highlanders an hour later and everyone had stopped for a much-needed break. Many of the Highlanders looked as if they were on their last legs.

"Two hours," said Anara, sitting on a rock next to Oso. She didn't like to be very far from him when he was around.

"That's too long," said Thomas. "Even with the rock slide, the reivers are no more than an hour behind us."

Extending his senses to locate the reivers had given Thomas a splitting headache and was almost too much for him. Kursool certainly was persistent. He had lost about a third to half of his forces to Thomas and Oso's latest ambush, yet he kept coming. Of course, if Thomas was in the same position himself, he'd be doing much the same.

Thomas organized his ragged group. The determination was there. He could see it in the eyes of the Highlanders. They had given everything they had left during the day, and still refused to give up, despite their weakness. Anara had done an excellent job, pushing them to their very limits. Unfortunately, it just wasn't enough.

"We'll have to fight a rearguard action, then," said Thomas, unable to think of any other solution. It would mean lives lost, but it could also lead to the freedom of many. "Those who are able to fight will retreat slowly and try to give the women, children and injured time to get to Raven's Peak."

"That won't be necessary, Thomas," said a soft voice from behind the rock on which Oso and Anara were sitting.

Thomas smiled. He had been waiting to hear that voice for quite awhile.

In a flash Oso was on his feet, sword in hand, having pulled Anara behind him. A tall man and a petite woman stood before him. The man was a head taller than he was, which unnerved him. He was the most intimidating person Oso had ever seen. There was a fire in his eyes that matched the one he had seen in Thomas' on occasion. How could these two have snuck up on him so quietly? It was unnatural. Oso felt a strong hand on his own, forcing his sword point to the ground. Thomas stood next to him.

"Oso, don't worry. These are my grandparents, Rynlin and Rya."

Oso stared at the two for a moment, still trying to figure out how they had appeared right behind him without any hint of movement or sound. "But how—"

Thomas gave his friend a meaningful look. "They taught me everything I know."

Oso nodded and slipped his sword back into its sheath. "Sorry about that," he said sheepishly.

"Completely understand," said the tall man, the one Thomas had named Rynlin. "We probably should have announced ourselves."

"You've been busy, Thomas," said Rya, stepping around the

rock to take a closer look at her grandson. He certainly did look the worse for wear. "Very busy indeed."

She knew he was exhausted and in a great deal of pain. But he stood there stoically, ignoring his injuries. She wanted to run over and hug him. But he was too old for that now and had been through too much. Rynlin was right. He had grown up faster than most. She regretted his having to do that, but as she had often told him, you must do what you must do.

"Busy," snorted Rynlin. "Looks like he's gotten himself into trouble again."

His grandson grinned at him in pride and Rynlin couldn't help but return the smile. Thomas looked just like a rogue, reminding Rynlin of himself.

"These Highlanders were forced to work in the mines," Thomas started to explain. "Oso and I have been trying to get them to safety, but we can't seem to get rid of the reivers behind us. We—"

"We know, Thomas," said Rya. "We got here as quickly as we could. We saw much of what was going on, even from our great distance."

Thomas had taken entirely too many risks, and she meant to have a word with him about that. She saw that Thomas understood her hidden meaning, and his grin disappeared.

"You and your friend there," said Rynlin, motioning to Oso, "make quite a pair."

"Thomas," said Rya. "Why don't you get everyone moving again. Rynlin and I will take care of things for you."

"But don't you need any help?" asked Anara. "Thomas said there were at least a hundred reivers still after us. I'm certain that most of the men here would be happy to—"

"Child, don't worry about us," said Rya. "We'll be able to handle things quite easily."

"But—"

Oso took hold of Anara's arm and pulled her toward the

rest of the group, many of whom were already rising to their feet having overheard snatches of the conversation.

"I'll explain it to you later, Anara. If Rya says she can take care of things, I wouldn't doubt her."

Anara gave Oso a withering look. She didn't like being manhandled, but she made no effort to remove her arm from his grasp. Yes, Thomas was right. His friend was in for more trouble than he knew. And when he realized what he had gotten himself into, it would probably be too late for him.

"Thank you," said Thomas. "If you hadn't shown up, I don't know what we would have done."

"It sounded like you had everything figured out, Thomas," said Rynlin. "We just wanted to get in on some of the fun."

"Now what are you doing still standing there," said Rya, placing her hands on her hips. "As I said, Rynlin and I will take care of it. You're too weak to be of any use to us right now anyway." She surveyed him with a critical eye and he winced under her inspection.

"Yes, grandmother," said Thomas resignedly. There was no arguing when Rya used that tone of voice.

"Now get going and we'll catch up to you later."

"Yes, grandmother."

Oso and Anara had already gotten the Highlanders back on their feet and headed deeper into the Highlands. Anara was once again in the lead, but this time Oso was with her, his hand still on her arm. He wondered how long it would take for his friend to figure out exactly what was going on. Thomas waited until the last of the Highlanders had passed him before following after the group. He certainly didn't envy what Kursool and his men were walking into. If they thought taking on Oso and him was frightening, just wait until he met his grandparents.

35

A COLD DISH

"So, what shall we do?" asked Rynlin, rubbing his hands together in anticipation.

Rya looked at him with a wicked gleam in her eye. "I think these reivers deserve a few more surprises."

Rynlin grinned. "I've always liked the way your mind worked, my love."

"Really," she said in mock surprise. "I always thought you married me because of my body."

"I did," replied Rynlin with a straight face. "Then with time I learned to love everything about you."

Rya took a playful swipe at her husband. "How did I ever fall for such a scoundrel?"

The fear of not knowing what had happened to her grandson had left her. He was all right, if a little worse for wear. She couldn't stop smiling. And best of all, she could exact her revenge upon those who had hurt him. She did not consider revenge to be a useful emotion, but giving in to it once in a while did wonders for the spirit.

"I don't know, my love. I really don't know." Rynlin offered his arm to his wife. "Why don't we go a little farther down the trail. When we were looking for a place to land I saw the perfect spot for our surprise."

"THERE THEY ARE," said Rynlin, peering down from a hill that was off to the side of the trail.

"Yes, I see them," replied Rya.

Thomas and Oso had done a very thorough job of whittling down the reivers pursuing them. Less than a hundred black-clad men had appeared at the edge of the forest and made their way out into the open, following after the Highlanders. Yes, Thomas and Oso had done an extremely thorough job. Most of the reivers kept scanning their surroundings as if they were about to be attacked. One of them finally pointed in the direction of the hill, having seen Rynlin and Rya standing there.

36

GROWING TREPIDATION

Who were those two? They certainly didn't resemble the two figures he had expected to see. Kursool used his hand to shield the sun from his eyes. A man and a woman. They couldn't do much harm to him and his men from where they were standing, he decided. Why were they watching him, though? Despite the distance, the pair made him feel like he was cornered with no chance of escape.

"Hold your fire," he yelled to his men. Several of the reivers had aimed their crossbows at the two; a few even fired. "They're too far out of range, you fools."

The reivers with crossbows realized their futility and lowered their weapons. It had taken Kursool more than an hour to get his men back together after the rockslide, what was left of them anyway. He was down to seventy-three men from the original three hundred he had started the day with, most dead, perhaps twenty running away in fear. He had not bothered going after them.

What were those two doing up there? Suddenly, the feeling of something being terribly wrong took hold of him again. He looked up the slope to see if any rocks were tumbling in his direction, but all was quiet. Nevertheless, he had ignored his sixth sense once today and paid the price for it. He would not do so again.

A rumble filled his ears, very much like the sound of thunder. Kursool glanced at the blue sky. There was not a cloud in sight. He had absolutely no idea what was going on. Worst of all, he had the terrible feeling that his luck had just run out.

37

DISPLAY OF POWER

"Have you found the leader?" asked Rya, peering down at the soldiers.

It was comical in a way. They watched the reivers and the reivers watched them. Unfortunately for the reivers, they didn't yet realize that instead of playing the role of the cat, as was their wont, Rynlin and Rya had assumed that character. Now, the reivers would be the mice.

"Yes, I've got him. Let's get started."

Rynlin and Rya took hold of the Talent, drawing on the great strength of nature. Each pulled in as much as possible, careful not to overstep the bounds of control. Once they had reached their limit, they opened themselves to each other and weaved their Talents together, combining their strength so they could pull in even more of the power of nature. The earth began to rumble beneath their feet, protesting at the energy they held within them, demanding that it be released. And release it they did.

A lightning bolt streaked down from the clear blue sky, incinerating Kursool and temporarily blinding the men around him. The reivers were too horrified by what they had just seen to move. A lightning bolt had shot down from a cloudless sky, turning their leader into ashes before their eyes. Then another lightning bolt struck the ground, destroying several more reivers, and another bolt followed.

The lightning bolts struck faster and faster, tearing up the earth in great chunks. Released from the spell they had been under, the reivers fled for the safety of the trees. What had been a simple mission at the beginning of the day had become one of personal survival. Yet, no matter how hard they tried to escape, the lightning bolts inevitably found them, leaving men torn and twisted, once live bodies now simply burned out husks.

It ended in a matter of minutes. Rynlin and Rya released their holds on the Talent. Quiet reigned in the Highlands once again. The only reminder of what had occurred was the scene that lay before them. The ground below was covered with holes deep enough to hide a man. In many cases they did.

"I don't think the reivers will be following after Thomas and the Highlanders any longer," said Rynlin, stating the obvious.

"I do believe you're correct, my love," said Rya, having quickly lost interest in the battlefield. They did not enjoy killing, and certainly not on such a large scale, but sometimes it was necessary. And admittedly, it had felt good to retaliate against the men who had taken their grandson from them.

"Why don't we catch up to Thomas and the others," suggested Rynlin. "I'd like to know how he got himself into this mess in the first place."

"An excellent idea," agreed Rya. "An excellent idea."

38

FAREWELL

"Are you sure you don't want to continue with us, Thomas?" asked Oso. "We're only a few miles away. There are many who will want to thank you for your help."

"I'm sorry, Oso. I can't. It's time for me to go."

Thomas didn't have the courage to explain his fear of meeting Coban once again. He felt like a coward, yet his heart told him he was doing the right thing. Now was not the time.

"I still owe you a debt, Thomas."

"You know, Oso, a great many people have been telling me that over the last few days. I'm getting tired of hearing it."

Oso laughed. "We are Highlanders, Thomas. You know how important something like this is to us."

"I know. I know." Thomas couldn't help but smile. "Well, then, to lessen the number of people who seem to feel they owe a debt to me, let me give you a task that will remove yours."

Oso stood a bit straighter, though it was clearly an effort because of his exhaustion. "Anything, Thomas. Just name it."

"I want you to take Anara as your wife."

"What—" Oso spluttered helplessly, shocked by the request.

Thomas laughed heartily. "I'm sorry, Oso. I'm just kidding. I couldn't help myself."

Oso looked greatly relieved. Thomas didn't doubt that if he had been serious, and Anara willing, Oso would have gone through with it. And Thomas had a feeling that Anara was more than willing. The way that she looked at Oso confirmed it. Whether Oso knew it or not, he had already found a wife. It was just a matter of time before he came to that conclusion as well.

"Have a safe trip," said Oso, taking hold of Thomas' hand.

"Thank you, my friend. Perhaps when I visit we can go hunting, if I can pry you away from Anara."

Oso flushed, scuffing his boot in the dirt from embarrassment. "An excellent idea, Thomas. An excellent idea."

Giving Oso a final wave, he walked to the edge of the trees where Rynlin and Rya waited for him.

"So young man," said Rynlin, "shall we head home and take a break from your adventures?"

"That sounds like a good idea, Rynlin."

"Are you strong enough to fly?" asked Rya. She was still concerned about his recovery from his wounds. Most had healed quickly, and in a few days only the scars would remain.

In response, Thomas walked deeper into the woods and took hold of the Talent. A few minutes later he flew high above the Highlands as a raptor, with two large hawks trailing behind him. As the currents of air flew past his feathers, he savored the freedom of flight, the freedom he had lost for too long a time.

39

DEMAND

"Why can't I learn the sword, Kael? You know I can do it. I'm already better with a dagger than any of the boys you're training now."

Kael balanced on his toes, knees flexed, watching Kaylie as she circled around him much like a cat before pouncing on an unsuspecting mouse. However, in this situation the cat didn't realize it was actually stalking a bear.

It was early evening, the sun lazily dropping toward the horizon. The smells of the kitchen drifted on the wind to the training circle situated in the far western corner of the Rock. It was not much to speak of really. Just a large dirt field surrounded by stone walls on two sides and benches on the other two, much of it now in shadow because of the time of day. But it served its purpose.

Kael had used it for twenty years to train the soldiers of Fal Carrach, and though some believed he was biased, he felt he could honestly say that there were no better fighters in any of the Kingdoms. Except the Highlands, of course. He was a Highlander first and foremost, so he allowed such prejudices.

Kael turned to face the Princess of Fal Carrach as she

searched for an opening in his defenses. She was persistent, sometimes annoyingly so, when she wanted something. What irritated him even more was that she was right. Kaylie surpassed his other students in the dagger. She was fast, very fast. But he still was the Swordmaster, and the best blade in Fal Carrach, and as such, he had a reputation to uphold. On this day he would. Kaylie was not ready to defeat him. Not yet, anyway. Soon, though, she might very well take him. She was that good, and with her persistence would only get better.

"Because your father said no," he reminded the princess.

His response had its desired effect. They practiced with wooden daggers, their tips covered in thick leather to prevent any injury. Blue chalk dusted the leather to confirm a successful strike. During the past half-hour, neither had scored a hit. Kael had not really bothered to attack. Instead he had tested his current pupil, looking for weak spots in her technique. So far he had found none. Until now. Kaylie's temper often got the better of her, and he had just found the right key for unlocking it.

"That's not fair! If I can learn to fight with a dagger, I should be able to do the same with a sword. Just because my father thinks girls shouldn't fight with a blade doesn't mean he's right."

Kaylie struggled to force out her words between breaths. Her exhaustion only added to her frustration. Kael had worked her hard during the session, which she appreciated. He always told her that she'd have to work harder than any of the boys to prove her true worth, and she had taken his words to heart. Yet there was a price to pay for that. Her long, black hair had become more of a nuisance as the duel progressed, the sweat-streaked strands clinging annoyingly to her forehead and swinging in front of her eyes, forcing her to flick them away with her free hand.

"Your father said no and that's the end of it," he answered harshly.

His words nudged the door to her anger open even farther. Kael had seen the signs — her indignant expression at being refused something, the angry glint in her eyes. Kaylie was very good with a dagger, but she had not yet learned how to keep her emotions in check. In a duel you had to remain calm and collected. Otherwise you died. It was that simple.

"But—"

"No buts, Princess. Your father said no. Now pay attention to what you're doing."

Kael saw his chance. Kaylie's rising anger made her movements less fluid. She clearly had lost her rhythm and concentration. Lunging forward with lightning speed, Kael caught Kaylie's dagger hand in his own and gently pressed his own dagger to her throat. The blue chalk on her neck ended the training session.

"You're dead, Princess."

Kaylie threw down her practice dagger in disgust, cursing as well as any soldier. She had been doing so well, only to lose because she had forgotten the most important thing Kael had taught her. Don't let anything break your concentration. How was she supposed to prove anything to her father if she didn't maintain her composure? Wanting to strike out at something, she kicked at the dirt, sending a cloud of dust into the air.

Kael ignored her display and walked toward the main hall. He was tired and hungry, and the smell coming from the kitchens promised an excellent dinner. Besides, if he didn't make his escape now, she'd want another chance at him.

"Pay attention to what you're doing, Princess. No matter how good you are with a blade, you only have to make one mistake to lose."

Kaylie watched the Swordmaster until he disappeared through a doorway, frustration plain on her face. He was right, of course. She knew that, but she didn't have to like it. Another lesson learned. Yet she had almost had him! A couple of times she had come very close to winning, missing with her lunges by a finger's breadth or less. She had done everything right, except stay focused on her task. She promised herself that she would not make the same mistake again.

"A very good show, Princess."

Kaylie jumped around, startled by the clapping. She always trained with Kael after he had finished with the recruits. She hadn't expected anyone else to be there. Maddan. Wonderful. Of all the people to watch her fail, it had to be him.

"What do you want, Maddan?"

"Nothing at all, Princess. Nothing at all." The blue-eyed boy walked right up to her. Too close for Kaylie's taste, she stepped away from him. Many girls at the Rock found his grin irresistible and swooned at the sight of his shoulder-length blonde hair. She was not one of them. "I was just watching. You're quite good with a dagger, Princess. Not as good as me, but still quite good."

Her anger burned hotter. There were only two people in the entire Rock better than her with a dagger: Kael and her father. Kael had said so himself, and he was not one to give such praise lightly. She took Maddan's bragging as an insult.

"That's a lie and you know it, Maddan. Now what do you want? I have better things to do than stand here and listen to your bragging."

In her opinion that's all he was really good for, as evidenced by his display, or lack thereof, in the Burren. As the son of Norin Dinnegan, Maddan was used to being treated with a certain deference. However, his father's wealth meant nothing to her, and Kaylie took particular delight in pointing out her lack of respect for him on a regular basis. It took Maddan several seconds to rein in his own anger before speaking. No matter how often she refused to acknowledge his standing, it still irritated him.

"So you want to be a warrior? You're such a pretty girl, Kaylie. Why would you want to do such a thing?"

Maddan was quite good at finding the holes in a person's armor. His jibe hit its mark.

"I will do as I please, Maddan."

"Of course, Princess. Of course. I didn't mean to imply anything. I was simply trying to point out that you should be thinking of marriage now, rather than being a soldier. There are many who would willingly have you as a wife." His arrogant sneer told her that Maddan was one of them.

Kaylie's eyes narrowed. She instantly saw Maddan in a whole new light, though she had known him for years. He was playing a new game now. A dangerous game. She knew he was greedy, but only just then realized the full extent of his avarice.

"I may be of an age to marry, Maddan, but I will not do so until I find the right person. And I have not found the right person." Kaylie bit off the last of her words as if she were chewing on leather, certain that he had picked up on her meaning. Turning her back to Maddan, she headed for her rooms.

Much to her surprise, a hand on her arm whipped her back around. She stood face to face with Maddan, no more than a few inches separating them.

"Don't walk away from me, Kaylie," he hissed through clenched teeth. "Perhaps you have found the right person, yes? You simply don't know it yet."

Kaylie refused to be intimidated. "You forget yourself, Maddan," she replied, her icy words barely a whisper, yet her fiery eyes spoke volumes. She was the Princess of Fal Carrach and would not be treated in such a way.

Maddan stared down in shock at the dagger pressed against his chest. A real dagger, and quite sharp. The point dug into his skin, drawing a few drops of blood. With one quick movement,

Kaylie could bury the blade in his heart. He immediately released her arm and tried to step away, but Kaylie moved with him, keeping the blade just above his heart.

Her father had bothered her countless times about carrying a dagger with her wherever she went, even going so far as to hide it under her gown if she were attending a feast or ceremony. Maybe if her father had witnessed how quickly she had turned the tables on Maddan his opinion of her learning to fight would change. Kaylie smiled wickedly.

"I will choose whoever I wish to marry, Maddan. But know this. It will never be you."

She pushed harder with her dagger to punctuate her words, the drops of blood turning into a slow trickle. Satisfied that she had made her point, literally, Kaylie resheathed her blade and walked toward the main keep.

"Next time, Maddan, I won't hesitate." She didn't bother to turn around.

40

PLAYING THE GAME

Inishmore was the largest kingdom in the west, dwarfing all its neighbors except Armagh. That's what drew Rodric to it. He craved power, and in Inishmore that's what he saw — an opportunity to increase his power. Twenty years before a group of lords had assassinated the doddering old fool who had been king. That action had turned the once peaceful kingdom into a den of vipers. Since then Inishmorian lords and ladies spent most of their time jockeying with one another for the chance to become king or queen. Yet no king or queen had sat on the throne in Laurag since the Good King Lassin met his untimely demise.

Oh, a handful of lords and ladies had succeeded in assuming the throne, yet none lasted for more than a few months at a time, some no more than a few days. Either their coalitions fell apart and they were forced to withdraw their claim or, more often, a competitor had them removed. Rodric saw it as the ultimate game of survival, playing in the politics of Inishmore. Over the years he had secretly supported a dozen or more claimants for the throne of Inishmore. Only one had survived, and the poison that some enterprising assassin had spread on the sheets of the fool's bed had turned the poor bastard's brain into so much mush he could no longer care for himself.

Still, despite his failures, Rodric played the game. Inishmore was a rich country, with Laurag functioning as the main port for distributing the highly prized silks and spices of the Distant Island. The Three Fork River offered a fast and cost-effective route for transporting these and other goods to Armagh and the Heartland Lake. Controlling the trade along the river had certainly enriched Rodric's coffers, and if he could take control of the country itself, whether openly or through an intermediary tucked safely into his pocket, his wealth would increase tenfold.

That's why the latest news from Laurag had upset him so much. He was a meticulous planner. When someone disrupted his strategies, he took it as a personal affront.

"I don't give a cow's ass what Eshel thinks of the treaty, Toreal," yelled Rodric, slamming his fleshy fist down on his desk, its top a smoothly polished wood with his likeness carved into the very center under a cover of glass. "We came to an agreement. He will do as the agreement requires."

Toreal watched his master carefully, ready to leap out of the way at a moment's notice. Rodric's temper was quite mercurial. As the bearer of bad news more often than not lately, Toreal had become particularly adept at dodging expressions of his master's anger, such as the gold goblet that had barely missed his head and slammed into the far wall just a few minutes before. Though Rodric's tantrums were common, they still unnerved him. Toreal repeatedly ran his hand through his short, bristly hair in consternation. Realizing what he was doing, he shoved his hands into the folds of his grey robes. As the Chamberlain of Eamhain Mhacha, his position demanded that he maintain the appearance of calm and control, even under the most trying of circumstances. And any circumstance that directly involved Rodric was always trying.

"I'm sorry, milord," said Toreal in a soothing voice. He used the same voice with his young children when they were upset, and it normally quieted them down. It had much the same effect on Rodric. "I can only relay what was said to me by the messenger sent by Lord Eshel. He truly appreciates your offers to assist him in gaining the throne of Inishmore, but if he had known that you would be stationing our troops on his properties in Laurag, he says he never would have agreed to it."

"He would have agreed to it, Toreal, if I required he sell his mother into slavery. He can't win the throne of Inishmore by himself. Without me, he's nothing but another hungry dog fighting with all the others over a very large bone."

"True, milord," replied Toreal in a more confident tone, pleased to see that his master had calmed down. "What shall I say in return?"

"You shall tell him quite simply that the agreement we signed still stands, and that if he does not adhere to it, he will no longer receive the gold he so desperately needs. Tell him also that I will relay to some of his closest friends in Laurag the details of our arrangement. As soon as they find out that he's essentially become my vassal in hopes of winning the throne, he won't live out the day. Tell him he'd then become the bone for all the other dogs to fight over. Tell him that, Toreal."

"Harsh words, milord."

"They are, Toreal, but necessary. He has a copy of our agreement. He should have read it before he signed it. It says quite clearly that in exchange for Armagh's gold he would allow me to quarter one hundred Armaghian soldiers on each of his properties in Laurag at his expense."

Eshel had in fact tried to read the entire agreement, but had been distracted by the wine Rodric continued to pour for him as they discussed the final details of the treaty. If nothing else,

Rodric was meticulous. He knew how to get what he wanted, and the easiest way to do that was to play upon his opponent's weaknesses. One of Eshel's many weaknesses just happened to be Ferranagh red wines.

"Without the law and the agreements made between Kingdoms and between persons, we would have nothing to hold our society together..."

Toreal listened to Rodric's lecture with one ear. He had heard the High King's rationalizations of his political actions many times before. Rodric loved having everything in writing, if for no other reason than to do what he was now doing to Eshel. At first the hypocrisy of Rodric's words had shocked Toreal, yet after hearing the same speech over and over, he no longer paid attention. Rodric adhered to an agreement only for as long as it suited him. Once it proved a hindrance, he would be the first to break it. Yet still Rodric expected others to follow their agreements with him to the letter, seeing their unwillingness to do so as a personal betrayal.

"Now leave me, Toreal. I have more important matters to attend to today."

"Yes, milord. I will relay your response at once." Bowing before turning on his heel, Toreal slipped out of the room and closed the door behind him, leaving Rodric in silence.

The High King leaned back into his chair and pulled the folds of his purple robes tighter around him. Dealing with a fool like Eshel was simple, and much like the bite of a mosquito — more of an annoyance than anything else. Dealing with his next visitor would prove more difficult, and much like the bite of a bloodsnake — deadly. He never relished these meetings, but it was the price he had to pay for getting what he wanted. As Rodric constantly reminded himself, the High King was to be feared and respected. Still, Rodric's next guest never failed to make him afraid.

41

A LESSON

Rodric realized at a very young age that there was little difference between a king and a common man besides the quirk of fate. Though that knowledge didn't please him, he could certainly put it to use. It was quite simple really. Power was based on perception. If you appeared to be a king, rather than a common man, then in most people's eyes you were a king. That had made life much easier for Rodric, since he didn't look like a king at all. The storybooks glorified kings such as Ollav Fola, whose shadow supposedly covered out entire armies. They spoke of his long blonde hair and striking features.

Rodric didn't have the long blonde hair or strong chin. His skin was splotchy rather than fair, and he had coarse black hair and a plain face. Worst of all — in his own opinion — he was short. Still, he soon discovered several ways to make up for his natural disadvantages.

As he paced in front of the Golden Throne of Eamhain Mhacha, he glanced nervously at his arrangements for the hundredth time. He had little to fear. The servants had learned long before that to fail in even the slightest task was to be avoided at all costs.

The throne room of Eamhain Mhacha, despite the rain that poured from the skies and struck heavily against the glass windows that ran from floor to ceiling, still shone brilliantly thanks to the hundreds of torches affixed to the walls. The pure white marble columns that rose to the ceiling reflected the light throughout the chamber. Even more impressive, the throne itself glowed liked the sun. The brightness appealed to Rodric. The aura of brilliance centered on him, giving him a dramatic sense of grandeur. The purple robe and large golden crown he wore to mark his station aided the deception.

Of course, his retainers and the hundred soldiers — silver breastplates shining brightly, their faces resembling the stone of the columns — who ringed the room only added to the effect. All in all, Rodric was rather pleased with his efforts. The nervousness that normally plagued him at times such as these had diminished. He actually felt comfortable for once. He was the High King of Eamhain Mhacha! No ruler was more powerful than he! Rodric's confidence disintegrated in a split second.

"Milord," said Toreal, having opened one of the massive doors to the throne room just enough to squeak through. "Lord Chertney."

The doors swung inward at a shocking speed. Toreal barely escaped being crushed as the two slabs of oak slammed against the walls, the boom echoing violently throughout the room and startling its occupants.

"Rodric," said a dark shadow standing on the threshold. "It was good of you to see me on such short notice."

Shivers of fear ran up and down Rodric's spine. Crawling beneath his throne and hiding passed through his mind. He hated the fact that he was afraid, and he hated the man who stood at the other end of his throne room even more for making him afraid. Rodric stepped back as the shadow strode into the room, but his heel ran into one of the legs of the throne. He had nowhere to go. In an attempt to retain his dignity, Rodric sat down in the golden chair.

Lord Chertney looked more like a king than Rodric ever would, and Chertney knew it. The tall, wraithlike man glided closer to Rodric, his eyes burning intensely, his posture speaking of power and dominance. The black leather armor he wore sucked in the light of the torches, creating a shadow that settled around him.

"I would like to speak with you alone, Rodric," said Chertney, coming to a halt just a few steps in front of the throne, his deep voice booming throughout the room. Though Rodric's throne sat on a dais, much to Rodric's chagrin Chertney still towered over him.

Rodric stared at the insolent smile on Chertney's face and the slicked back hair. The swine! Rodric fought hard to maintain his composure. How dare he enter his throne room without permission! How dare he call the High King of Armagh by his first name! How dare he tell him, Rodric, what to do! Though his face turned red with anger, he replied in a calm voice.

"Lord Chertney, it is a pleasure to have you with us once again. I'm sure that whatever you wish to discuss can be heard by those here with us."

More than anything else, Rodric wished desperately not to be left alone with this man. If he truly was a man. The soulless eyes made him wonder. Rodric's kind, composed words did not have their desired effect.

"I will speak with you alone, Rodric," hissed Chertney, his eyes blazing red with anger. "If you won't clear the room, I will do it myself."

A cold sweat ran down Rodric's back as he gazed into those eyes. It was rumored that Chertney drank the blood of the men he killed in battle to absorb their strength. Rodric had dismissed the story as just that, a story. Now, staring into those eyes, he believed them. Knowing that having Chertney order his people to leave his throne room only would increase Rodric's humiliation, he tried to save face.

"I can see, Chertney, that you must have a matter of great import to discuss with me," he said with some composure, though he seethed inside. "As you wish then. Toreal, please clear the room."

"Yes, milord," answered Toreal, who had walked a good distance away from the doors, just to be safe.

The soldiers and retainers in the throne room didn't need much urging to leave. In less than a minute Chertney had his wish, the doors slamming shut just as Toreal stepped through.

The throne room that had glowed so brightly just moments before now took on a gloomy cast. The fear that tickled Rodric's spine settled in his stomach. He clenched the armrests of the throne, desperately trying to keep his hands from shaking.

"So, Chertney, you have your private audience," said Rodric.

Chertney raised an eyebrow. The false confidence in Rodric's voice appeared comical to him.

"This is not an audience," began Chertney, stepping on to the platform, his voice traveling to the farthest corners of the room with ease. "This is a lesson, Rodric. How are things progressing in the east?"

Rodric put on his most ingratiating smile. "Everything goes as planned. In just a few years, by law, the Highlands will be mine. But until then, our strategy has worked out quite well. The time for the next step approaches, and we will be ready."

Inwardly, Rodric cursed Killeran for an incompetent fool. He had given Killeran everything he needed — men, supplies, money — and more, and still he sent only a trickle of the wealth rumored to lie within those cursed mountains. How was he supposed to pursue his plans when—

Chertney's face darkened like a thundercloud. To him, Rodric was a weakling who had absolutely no idea what he was doing. He was a bug, and the only thing a bug was good for was being stepped on. Yet his master forbid it, for now. Though Chertney didn't understand why, he knew better than to dispute his master's decisions.

"What about the Lost Kestrel?"

"The what?" asked Rodric. "I don't understand."

"Of course you don't, Rodric. You're a fool. What about the Lost Kestrel?"

The insult failed to register. Rodric had heard that term before, but from whom? His confusion was obvious.

"The Lost Kestrel?"

Chertney ignored Rodric. "It is rumored that the grandson of Talyn Kestrel survived the attack on the Crag and has been hiding in the Highlands ever since. At first I thought it was just a story, created by the Highlanders as a way to keep their spirits up. I'm not so sure anymore."

"Yes, I've heard something of that as well," said Rodric, trying to appear knowledgeable. "It is nothing to worry about, Chertney. You're afraid of ghosts. The grandson died just like his—"

Chertney's withering glare pushed the High King back in his chair. "Just because it is a rumor does not make it false." Rodric cringed at the harshness of Chertney's tone. "Most rumors have a kernel of truth. The grandson's body was never found after the Crag fell. I know. I was there. I destroyed the Crag and turned over every piece of rubble looking for the boy."

"But that doesn't mean he escaped," protested Rodric.

The task for eliminating the Kestrel line had fallen to Rodric after Chertney destroyed the Crag, who had in turn left the matter in Killeran's hands. Yet, if Killeran's skills as Regent of the Highlands were any sign, it was entirely possible that he could have failed in that as well. He couldn't admit to that possibility, though. The ally who had given him that task did not tolerate failure. "He probably died like his father and grandfather as Rodric suggested. His body simply was never found. The forest in that part of the Highlands is extremely dense and almost impassable in certain areas."

"I used to think much the same, Rodric," said Chertney. "But I have been hearing some new, disturbing rumors originating from the Highlands. I have heard of a man or a beast — no one knows for sure — who is systematically eliminating the servants of our master when they walk in the Highlands. The Highlanders call him, or it, the Raptor. Though no one can say exactly what this creature is, they all agree on one thing. Do you know what that is, Rodric?"

Rodric wished desperately that he had the answer, but could only mumble incoherently. His hands began to shake again, and though he clenched the armrests with all his might, it didn't help.

"Green eyes, Rodric. Green eyes that blaze in the night." Chertney leaned over Rodric to emphasize his point, and the tall man's imposing frame loomed over the High King, placing him in shadow. "Did you know, Rodric, that the grandson of Talyn Kestrel had green eyes? Green eyes that supposedly blazed in the night?"

"Yes, well, that still doesn't mean the rumor is true," stammered Rodric, looking for a way to escape Chertney's gaze. With Chertney standing in front of him, his throne now resembled a prison. "Many boys have green eyes—"

"Yes, that is true, Rodric. I offer additional evidence. After the Crag fell, and the body of the grandson was never found, our master sent several of his other servants in pursuit, in case the boy survived. These servants have not found him during all the years they have searched, and these servants do not fail. They simply can't fail."

Rodric immediately picked up on Chertney's implication of his futility, but wisely chose to ignore the barb.

"My last bit of evidence: Your Regent captured a boy with green eyes. Despite my express order that I be notified if ever a green-eyed boy were to be taken, I never was." Chertney stepped back from Rodric, giving him room to breathe once again. "Last I heard, the boy had escaped, and during his escape, had burned down the fort that served as Killeran's headquarters."

Rodric leaped to his feet in shock. "The fort burned—"

"To the ground," answered Chertney. "Nothing is left. And from what I also hear, the Highlanders eliminated a large portion of Killeran's reivers during all the excitement."

Rodric slumped back down in his chair, his mind too numb to take it all in. The fort destroyed? How was he supposed to mine the Highlands without the fort? He needed more gold and silver than ever before. Otherwise his plans would come to a halt.

"This boy with green eyes may be no one at all. Then again, considering the amount of trouble he has caused, and the fact that rumors of this Lost Kestrel persist, I think it would be well worth your while to make sure this rumor truly is a rumor. Do you understand what I am telling you, Rodric?"

"Yes," mumbled Rodric. "Yes, I understand perfectly. The boy with green eyes will be found. I will take care of it myself."

"You have restored my confidence," said Chertney, his sarcasm plain. "I suggest you get started right away. As soon as you have captured him, notify me. Remember, Rodric, our master is not one who accepts failure."

Chertney's words chilled Rodric to the bone. He felt as if he were standing knee deep in snow, his legs stuck in place, with a freezing wind tearing at his clothes and turning parts of his body to ice. For the thousandth time, he rethought his decision to serve the master Chertney spoke of, yet knew in his heart that it was too late. Once you made such an alliance, there was no turning back. You either succeeded or died.

42

A NEW PLAYER

The palace of Eamhain Mhacha was the largest in all the Kingdoms, containing miles of hallways that connected thousands of rooms and chambers — some known, some not. Corelia Tessaril waited several minutes before pressing the hidden latch that released the wall, which allowed it to swing smoothly into the hall right in front of her father's private chambers. The suite of rooms behind the throne room was reserved for the High King and his family. No one was allowed there without express permission, even the servants, so she had little fear of discovery. Still, it was better to be cautious than bold.

Stepping out of the cubbyhole carved into the wall directly behind the throne of the High King, Corelia brushed a thin coating of dust from her dress as the wall swung back in place. Her father had just bought it for her — a deep blue velvet with a tight bodice and flowing skirts. It had cost a fortune, but as her father liked to say, nothing was too good for the daughter of the High King. Of course, she took full advantage of her father's largesse, for she knew the true reason behind his generosity.

Her father did not provide her with the best clothes strictly out of the goodness of his heart, though he would never admit to it. Corelia had observed the political games played in the hallways of the Armaghian palace. Power ruled here, and there were many ways to gain and manipulate it, as well as lose it.

Beauty was just one. Corelia's long blond hair flowed to her waist, and her eyes were a smoky blue. They fit perfectly with her sultry voice. Though she was barely an adult, she had many admirers, and Rodric played that card cleverly and without a second thought. But that was all right with her. Corelia knew that she was beautiful, and she knew how to use it to her advantage. More important, she knew how to play the game of power. She had been playing it all her life, both for and against her father.

She knew much of her father's plans already, thanks to her many hiding places. Yet today's meeting with Lord Chertney offered a new and tasty tidbit of information. One that could prove profitable, if she could figure out how to make use of it. She bit down on her lower lip, hands on hips and one foot in front of the other, deep in thought. It was a pose that most men found irresistible.

The Lost Kestrel, she murmured to herself. She imagined what he might look like — probably tall, with broad shoulders and a confident grin. A man to be reckoned with. A man of power, and perhaps a way to power. The idea of his possible existence intrigued her. Her father wanted the Highlands for the riches it contained. Perhaps she could gain those riches for herself. Men wanted power, but they also wanted something else. Something that only she could give them, if they were so fortunate.

She had heard stories of the Lost Kestrel and his many exploits. Though she had enjoyed their telling, she had never put much faith in the stories. But if Lord Chertney was so concerned about a myth, perhaps it wasn't a myth after all. This

Lost Kestrel sounded like a strong-willed man. She certainly would enjoy taming him.

"Daydreaming, Corelia?"

The question startled her, and she jumped back a step, almost hitting her head against the wall behind her. Anger filled her, and she was about to release a scathing reprimand on the person who had dared disturb her, until she saw who that person was.

"What are you doing in the private residence, Lord Chertney?" she asked smoothly, hiding her shock at his presence. "I'm sure you're aware that my father does not allow anyone here without his express permission."

Her voice was true royalty – one that was used to giving commands. Her indignation simply washed over Chertney, having little effect. His black eyes focused intently on the young woman in front of him. Corelia tried to maintain contact with those eyes, but found that she couldn't and lowered her gaze.

Chertney smiled. A strong one, this girl, but still malleable. Strength was good when used properly. He could have tested her in other ways, but he didn't have the time. Yet, he still wanted to find out if his initial estimate of her was correct.

"I have never met a spy as beautiful as you, Corelia. You have immeasurably enhanced a profession often looked upon with contempt by others."

Corelia's face turned red in shame. She had been found out. But how could he have known? Maybe he didn't. Maybe he was just guessing. Besides, this was her palace. She became a picture of cool serenity and strength, refusing to show her fear.

"I know nothing of what you say, Lord Chertney. As I said before, no one is allowed within these hallways without my father's express permission. I am quite certain, Lord Chertney, that you do not have that permission. I suggest you leave."

The acid in this young vixen's words made Chertney grin even more, the smile giving his sallow, dark features a ghoulish cast. He was correct. This one could be of use. Not yet. No, definitely not yet. But soon.

"As you wish, Corelia," answered Chertney smoothly, bowing at the waist and turning on his heel in one smooth motion. He was several steps away when he turned back around. "Remember one thing, though, Princess. Once you have turned down a certain road, often you cannot go back. I suggest you choose your path wisely."

The tall, dark man strode down the hallway, his frame disappearing into the shadows created by the torches lining the walls. In the blink of an eye, he was gone.

Corelia stood there for several minutes, trying to regain her composure. Chertney's words made her feel as if someone had dumped a bucket of cold water on her, sending chills through her body. It was several minutes more before those chills finally disappeared.

43

A SECOND MEETING

Norin Dinnegan's head whipped around as the howl of a wolf ripped through the dark silence. On most nights such a sound would not have startled him. But this wasn't a normal night. The cold wind whipped across his face, forcing him to adjust his cloak for the hundredth time since he reached his latest place of commerce. He preferred standing by the warm fire of his private study and conducting his business the way he wanted. But his latest partner followed his own set of rules. Rules that Norin had no choice but to honor.

He scanned the forest glade once again. His troop of hired soldiers remained at their posts, an impenetrable circle at the edge of the small clearing. Nothing moved but the wind. They had left his mansion an hour before midnight, making their way northwest until they reached the very edge of the Burren. It was a strange place for a meeting, as well as dangerous. Most people avoided the Burren during the day if possible; no one willingly entered it at night.

Dinnegan guessed that it was several hours before dawn – he'd been waiting for more than an hour — though he couldn't tell for sure. Dark clouds hung in the sky, hiding the moon and stars. Even with the heavy wool cloak pulled tight around his shoulders, he shivered. However, he refused to admit to himself that the cause was anything but the cold. Besides the occasional wolf howl, silence reigned in the Burren. That's what made him and his men uncomfortable. Forests were active places at night, becoming quiet only when predators prowled. In any other forest, man was the primary hunter. But in the Burren, even if only on the edge, man often became the prey.

Fear and anticipation mingled in his blood. He was the richest man in Fal Carrach, in fact in all the Kingdoms, yet his wealth no longer satisfied him. He wanted more. And as he had learned in his forty years of business, many times to achieve what you wanted you had to go outside the accepted channels of commerce.

"Well met, Dinnegan." The raspy voice emanated from a shadow standing just a few feet in front of him.

Dinnegan jumped back in fear. The voice drew the attention of his men, many of whom reached for their swords. He waved them off.

"Who are you?" asked Dinnegan, trying and failing to keep a tremble of fear from his voice.

The shadowy man had slipped past his guards with ease. Even now, when Dinnegan looked directly at the dark shape, he had difficulty picking it out from the blackness of his nighttime surroundings.

"You may call me Malachias." The crackly voice set Dinnegan's teeth on edge. "My master says everything is ready. The task will be done."

The shadowy man stepped forward, the sinuous, graceful movement lost to the eye. Dinnegan desperately wanted to run, sensing the creature's evil. Every part of his being told him to run, but he couldn't. Not if he wanted to complete this deal. "My master wishes to know what you will give him in return."

Dinnegan licked his lips before replying, desperate for a

swig of wine. His throat had suddenly gone dry. His response now would either make or break the deal. "Mountains of gold and other riches—"

"My master has no need for such things," hissed Malachias contemptuously. "Gold and jewels mean nothing to him."

"Then what?"

Dinnegan had never before had such an offer refused. Greed was a natural part of man's character. He didn't know what more he could offer. Dinnegan suddenly realized to his terror that he had horribly miscalculated. This wasn't just another business deal. His prospective partner demanded more.

"He wants you, Dinnegan." The chilling words burrowed into Dinnegan's heart. The small voice inside his head again told him to run, to forget this arrangement and escape. Yet his overwhelming ambition locked his feet in place. "My master will do as you wish, and you will gain what you desire, but in return you will serve him — doing as my master commands, when he commands."

Dinnegan stared at the dark shadow, for the first time in his life not knowing what to do. His fear, forgotten once the negotiations had begun, returned in full force. Could he make such an agreement, without knowing what the consequence might be? Was there any other way to gain what he wanted? Was there? If not, then was he willing to pay such a price? His greed and common sense battled within him. The fight lasted several minutes, but as it had so many times before, his avarice won out.

"So be it."

He tried to make his words ring strong, but to his ears they sounded hollow. For the first time in his life, he felt unsure of himself.

"So be it," replied the shadowy man, satisfied. "In a short time you will have what you desire."

With his task complete, Malachias disappeared into the night. Dinnegan spun around, looking for any sign of movement, but finding nothing. Not even in the thick dewy grass. Dinnegan's feet had flattened the long stalks all around him, but there was no sign of the messenger's passage. His soldiers weren't even aware that the meeting had ended.

Dinnegan remained where he was for almost an hour, lost in thought. He had gotten into several business contracts in the past, and out of just as many with nary a scratch. The cold wind blew over him, and this time he welcomed it. Sweat had formed on his forehead. Hopefully, he could do the same with this one when the time came. However, the small voice that had previously warned him to run now told him it was too late. In his heart, he knew the voice spoke true.

44

A WELCOME TASK

Thomas splashed into the water, trudging the last few feet to the shore and pulling the small sailboat up onto the beach. The calm of the early morning remained, the sun not yet touching the horizon. Soon, though, the animals and birds of the Highlands would awake, much to Thomas' delight.

"Come on, you coward." Beluil sat majestically on his haunches in the prow of the small skiff, not yet ready to disembark. He grinned wickedly at Thomas, showing his sharp teeth. "Your majesty need no longer fear getting his paws wet."

Thomas' sardonic tongue was lost on Beluil, as the large black wolf leapt onto the sand. He ran off to the edge of the tree line while Thomas dragged the boat farther up the beach, hiding it among the rocks and trees to prevent discovery. After wiping their tracks clean in the sand, he grabbed his pack and bow and followed his friend into the forest.

It was good to be back. Rya had argued that it was too soon, that he had not fully recovered from his wounds, as it had only been six weeks since his escape from the reivers. For Thomas it was not soon enough. Though still sore in several places, only the scars remained of his time in the Black Hole. Now the only pain he felt came when he looked in the mirror as his chest and back displayed the artistry of a whip and a poker. Just looking at the crisscrossing marks made him grimace in distaste. He could only imagine what someone else might think.

During the last few weeks he had argued repeatedly with his grandparents. Images of his people suffering in the mines never left him, nor did his feeling of helplessness. He had to do something, but each time he considered declaring himself the Highland Lord, Rynlin and Rya harshly called him a fool. In time he would return to take his grandfather's place. He had to wait until then. If he went back before he was ready, however, they told him that he would fail, and with him would die the hopes of his people.

At first, Thomas thought his grandparents were simply speaking out of fear, which was to be expected considering what he had just experienced. But he quickly discarded that notion. Rynlin and Rya weren't trying to protect him as they had before. They had realized during his captivity that they could no longer treat him like a child. Instead they wanted to help him. So Thomas wisely heeded their warning.

Of course, that didn't mean he had to stay within the confines of the Isle of Mist. No, he could still do something to help his people. So Thomas decided that he would continue to perform the duties required of a Sylvan Warrior, and perhaps add a task or two, such as preventing the reivers from putting any more of his people to work in the mines.

With Beluil trotting along at his side, he and the large wolf dodged among the trees, heading in a southwesterly direction toward where the Burren met the Highlands. It was as good a place as any to start his search. Reaching out for the Talent, Thomas let the familiar feeling rush through his body, then focused his attention on the surrounding forest. The bustle of activity hidden beneath the veil of calm comforted Thomas. In his mind he watched the ants carrying bits of food back to their hole, the woodpeckers searching for bugs in the trees, and the otters swimming in the Southern River.

They traveled in companionable silence for several hours, Beluil running off occasionally on a whim, but always returning to his friend's side. Thomas had relayed to the black wolf as much as he could about what had happened the last time he had ventured into the Highlands. Since then, Beluil had stayed close. So close in fact that the two had been virtually inseparable. They were almost to the edge of the Burren when Thomas stopped abruptly. Beluil watched his friend in anticipation, knowing what was to come.

Thomas stood transfixed for several seconds, neither speaking nor blinking. A faraway look entered his eyes. Finally, he came out of the trance, his calm expression replaced by one of purpose. He relayed what he had sensed to Beluil. *Evil. Wrongness. In the forest. Many evil. Quick death. Blood. Death. Fear. Scent of fear. Fearhounds. Fearhounds. Fearhounds!*

Beluil howled with fury. Wolves had no love for dark creatures, and the only thing they hated more than Ogren were Fearhounds. Thomas adjusted the pack on his shoulder, holding his sword in one hand and his bow in the other. He ran through the forest, easily sidestepping the trees that loomed up to block his way. Beluil followed closely at his heels. Their passage was barely noticeable, their quick movement seemingly no more than a slight breeze. The pack of Fearhounds was far to the north. He and Beluil would have to push hard, yet neither cared as they grinned in anticipation. The chase had begun.

45

VARIOUS TACKS

Gregory had hoped for a nice quiet day with his daughter, free of the everyday demands made on him. Yet quiet days were few and far between, even when traveling along the edge of the Burren. The troop of twenty soldiers marching around them ensured that. As the King of Fal Carrach he could do almost anything he pleased, but taking a few days to be alone with his daughter was not one of them.

Kael almost had a fit when Gregory told him he was only planning to take five soldiers with him. The Highlander finally relaxed when Gregory promised to take a full troop. Even then Kael was barely satisfied. He had mentioned the increasing number of reports coming back from the west and north about dark creatures roaming the border region. There was also more talk of this Raptor, who could be either friend or foe. Still, such rumors would not keep Gregory from his objective.

Lately, he had been spending more and more time on the affairs of state, due mostly to that uppity, weak-willed power monger playing at High King. A day didn't seem to go by without discovering some new scheme directed at Fal Carrach that was hatched jointly by Rodric and his sidekick, Loris of

Dunmoor. And that wasn't the worst of it. At least that was something he could deal with competently.

Women were an entirely different matter. Sarelle, Queen of Benewyn, had sent a formal correspondence — several in fact — asking Gregory to visit. Sarelle was a remarkably beautiful woman, her auburn hair blazing in the sunlight, her sharp, green eyes full of mischief. But that's what worried him. When Sarelle even glanced at him, his face became red and his palms sweaty. Though he was a king, he felt like a tongue-tied boy in her presence.

He had thanked her for the invitation, but respectfully declined, noting several pressing matters that required his attention. Much to his surprise she wrote back saying that she understood. Instead she'd visit him! Now what was he supposed to do? He had pondered that question for most of the morning, until Kaylie started in on him once again.

Ruling a kingdom was simple compared to raising a daughter too much like yourself. A daughter he had seen much too little of in recent weeks. Hence, his idea to patrol Oakwood Forest for a few days to be with her, and perhaps find a solution to his problem with Sarelle without embarrassing himself.

"Really, father, I just don't understand why you're being so stubborn," declared Kaylie, striding along next to her father in a linen shirt and tight-fitting breeks, her always-present dagger at her belt.

She had tried many different approaches in her argument with him so far today, from pleading to begging to demanding. Now she was trying to reason with him. As he looked down at his daughter, he saw her mother — long, raven black hair, deep blue eyes, a beautiful smile and the tenacity of a bulldog.

"I may be the daughter of a king, but that should not keep me from learning how to fight with a sword. As a woman, you never know when such knowledge might prove useful."

Her tone sounded rational, but her eyes spoke of something

else — irritation. Her father was probably the most obstinate man she knew. Nothing she had tried so far had worked. It just wasn't fair. So what if she was a woman. That should have no bearing on her learning how to fight with a blade.

A woman. Gregory had to admit his daughter was right. She was no longer a girl. But it was so hard for him to think of her as anything else. He remembered when she used to come running into the throne room covered in dirt from playing in one of the gardens, ordering him to come with her at once so she could go for a pony ride. She had last done that years ago, but it seemed like only yesterday. Of all the traits she had to inherit from him, why did it have to be his obstinacy?

"You're absolutely correct, Kaylie. I shouldn't treat you like a child. You're a woman now and should be treated as such." She missed the sly smile that crept onto his face.

"Thank you for coming to that realization, father."

Maybe all her efforts were finally going to pay off. Even the strongest of men wore down after hours of constant wheedling.

"In fact, it probably is time to start your training."

"Oh, father, thank you so—"

"I'll talk with Elissa as soon as we get back."

Kaylie's smile became a look of confusion. Elissa? What did Elissa have to do with learning the sword?

"Don't you mean Kael, father?"

"Kael? What does he have to do with this?" replied Gregory, doing his best to keep an even tone.

"But Kael's the Swordmaster. Why would Elissa teach me how to use a sword?"

"She wouldn't," answered Gregory, quickly scanning the forest around them and making sure his men were where they were supposed to be. The habits of a soldier died hard. "She'll be teaching you the six gifts of womanhood, passed down from the ancients: beauty, voice, sweet speech, needlework, wisdom and chastity. As a young woman, you need to know how to act properly, and Elissa is just the right person to teach you."

Caught completely off guard, Kaylie looked up at her father dumbstruck. The six gifts of womanhood? Where had he come up with that? Noticing a few more streaks of grey in the hair by his temple, the strands confirmed her suspicions. He was either growing senile or having fun at her expense. Well, two could play at that game.

"Excellent, father, I can hardly wait. But I think five is plenty. Chastity is such a tired, obsolete concept in this day and age."

"What?" Her father looked like he was going to swallow his tongue in shock. It took him a few seconds to realize that now he was on the receiving end. His shock quickly turned to irritation. Why was his daughter so exasperating? As soon as she bit on to something, she never let go. "All right, enough of that."

Kaylie refused to give in. "Why can't I learn to fight, father? Just because I'm a girl? That's just not right."

"It's not because you're a girl, Kaylie. It's because you're a princess." Gregory sighed in frustration. "I've told you that many times before."

"But all the boys my age are learning how to fight. Please, father, you know I can do it. Kael says I'm good enough with a dagger to take part in the competition at the Eastern Festival, and that's just a few months away. In fact, he says I'm better than any of the boys he's training now."

"Yes, but they're training to be soldiers. You're not. You're a princess, and someday you will be queen. As a result, you have certain responsibilities to the Kingdom and to your people. Learning how to fight with a sword is not one of those responsibilities."

"But what about me? What about what I want to do? Doesn't that matter?" Kaylie's voice cracked in desperation.

While growing up she had done almost anything she

wanted. Recently, though, she had learned that as a princess, you often faced more restrictions than freedoms.

"There are times when you must put the interests of your people, the people you are responsible for, before your own." Gregory tried to control his temper, but Kaylie had pushed him too hard. "You have gotten your way for far too long, Kaylie, and for that I blame myself. Perhaps if your mother were here, things would be different."

A tinge of sadness crept into his voice. "You are a princess, and you must learn how to rule Fal Carrach. I didn't raise you to be a spoiled brat, so stop acting like one. You will do as I say, and that's the end of it."

Gregory marched forward toward one of his soldiers. He hated having to put his foot down, but sometimes it was necessary. It was not the way he wanted to start the day, and hopefully didn't bode ill for the rest of it. All he had wanted to do was to spend a few days with his daughter in relative peace and quiet. Instead, he had walked into the middle of a maelstrom.

The end of it, was it, Kaylie fumed. The end of it! We'll see about that. Her father might think the argument over, but it wasn't. Not by a long shot. Taking a few moments to gather her thoughts and plan her next line of attack, Kaylie studied the foliage around her. They walked along a woodsman's trail barely wide enough for two people to travel abreast. She smiled every so often as an animal poked its head out from the bushes to see who intruded in its territory. First a squirrel, next a rabbit, then even a red fox.

The forest was absolutely remarkable, in her opinion. True, she was a princess, and had people to help her do whatever was needed, from picking out her clothes to starting her bath. Yet, there were the countless court functions as well, from having to receive lecherous, old ambassadors who lied through their teeth to sitting through the most mundane, boring feasts for hours on end. What she would give for just a few days of freedom — to decide what she was going to do, when she was going to do it and how.

The stone blocks of the Rock in recent months had begun to feel like cell walls. It was strange, really. The Rock was her home. Yet at times all she wanted to do was escape — from the Rock, from her responsibilities, from her life as a princess. Kaylie smiled as her imagination drifted in a dozen different directions. She wanted excitement. She wanted adventure. She wanted romance. Kaylie glanced at her father's back, just a few feet in front of her.

For one strange second, she thought she might have voiced what she was thinking, but she hadn't, thankfully. If she had, the shouting match they had just engaged in would have been nothing more than a quiet conversation compared to the inevitable argument to follow. Try as he might, her father refused to see her as anything but a little girl.

"You know, father, I learned something very interesting just the other day during one of my history lessons."

"Oh, what was that?" Gregory whispered a silent thank you, glad that Kaylie had finally decided to talk of something else.

"It had to do with the Highlands," she began, picking up her pace so she walked by his side again. When she got there, she gave her father her sweetest smile. She had watched him interact with other rulers and ambassadors. He would treat them with the greatest respect and utmost kindness, even if they insulted him. Then, when they were feeling comfortable and in control, her father would hit them like you would a stake with a sledgehammer, taking command of the situation with the sudden change in momentum and making his own demands, which were usually agreed upon. "The first Highland Lord was not a Lord after all."

"What do you mean by that?" he asked.

"Exactly what I said, father," said Kaylie, walking along

beside him. "The first Highland Lord wasn't really a lord." She knew she had piqued his interest.

"All right, out with it girl. I can't remember my history. How can the first Highland Lord not really be a lord? You mean he was a commoner?"

"No, not at all, father. The first Highland Lord wasn't a he, but a she, so obviously she couldn't be a lord. Her name was Alessandra, and when the clans of the Highlands gathered to choose their first Highland Lord, everyone assumed that it would be a man. But it didn't work out the way they thought it would.

"To become the Highland Lord the leaders of the different clans had to take a series of tests. The lord of one of the clans — I can't remember his name right now, but he's not important anyway — had died in a skirmish with Ogren. Because of that Alessandra, the dead clan lord's wife, took his place according to their laws until the clan chose a successor. But they didn't have time to select one because all the clans had to reach the gathering, so Alessandra went as the clan lord.

"Anyway, there were many different tests that the clan leaders had to pass, from reciting the history of the Highlands to fighting the best of the Highland champions to knowing the intricacies of the law. She passed all those tests without any trouble at all, but most of the other clan leaders failed. The last test was one of weapons. The clan leaders who remained, I think six or seven in all plus Alessandra, entered the training circle, and the last one to remain standing without being cut would be declared the first Lord of the Highlands. Obviously no one expected Alessandra to survive the competition.

"But she won!" The excitement in Kaylie's voice was tangible, bringing a wary smile to Gregory's face. He knew exactly where she was going with her story, but he didn't want to interrupt. If nothing else, it was good to know that she at least paid attention to some of her lessons.

"It just so happened that she was an only child, her mother having died when she was a baby. Her father didn't really know how to raise a girl all by himself, so he had taught her how to fight with a dagger, a sword and a bow. That training was put to good use. By the end of the competition she was the last one standing in the training circle without a drop of blood somewhere on her body. As a result, she was declared the first Highland Lord. So the first Highland Lord wasn't really a lord after all. And because of her, from that time forward, Highland women trained to become warriors just like the men."

"An excellent story, Kaylie," said Gregory. "I'm glad to see that you enjoy at least a few of your lessons."

"Yes, a very few," she said in frustration. Was her father really that dense? "Don't you see my point? If the women of the Highlands can learn how to fight, so can I. Alessandra was the ruler of the Highlands. I will rule Fal Carrach some day. It only seems appropriate that I should—"

"Enough, Kaylie," said Gregory, chopping the air with his hand to emphasize his point. "Enough. Despite your story, my opinion remains the same."

Kaylie stared at her father with daggers in her eyes. She mimicked her father chopping his hand through the air, mouthing the word "enough," but making sure that he couldn't see her while she did it. He was the most stubborn—

Fine, he still refused to teach her the sword. The trip wasn't over yet, and she could be just as stubborn as he, even more so. By the time they returned to the Rock, she'd have what she wanted.

"So what do you think about this Raptor, father?" Kaylie asked sweetly, though her eyes failed to match her voice. Try as she might, her irritation remained. "You know, the man, or animal, or whatever, that hunts the Highlands for the creatures of darkness. I keep hearing a new story every week about how this Raptor saved a small farmhouse from a band of

Fearhounds or protected a lone woodsman from Ogren. Just the other day a farmer told Kael that he had stumbled upon the still warm bodies of a Shade and a half-dozen Ogren in one of his fields. So what do you think, father?"

"I think you should spend less time listening to far-fetched stories."

"They might not be stories, father. Exaggerations, perhaps, but there's always a kernel of truth in every story. You told me that once, you know."

"Maybe," he replied noncommittally, "But I put little faith in the stories I hear about this Raptor. Some of it is just too remarkable to believe."

Kaylie thought about it for a moment and decided that her father might be right. Then again, he was wrong about not letting her learn the sword so he could be wrong about this as well.

"I wonder if the Raptor is the Lost Kestrel."

Gregory stopped abruptly and spun around. "Why do you think that?"

The sharpness of his voice surprised her. She hesitated before answering.

"I don't know, I was just thinking out loud. That's all."

Gregory grunted and walked ahead, obviously wanting to be alone with his thoughts.

Kaylie wondered what had gotten into him. She had never seen him act like that before. Oh, well, she'd think about that later. She still had to figure out how to convince him that he was being a bull-headed fool for not letting her train with Kael, but in a way that wouldn't result in a shouting match.

46

GETTING CLOSER

"Yes, Beluil, I know," said Thomas between breaths, translating the image sent by his friend. "I think they will come back too, and very soon."

They had tracked the pack of Fearhounds for most of the day and were still no closer to their quarry. Each time Thomas and Beluil angled in a direction that would allow them to catch up to the dark creatures, the pack moved off another two or three leagues.

Thomas blamed it on bad luck. The Fearhounds couldn't know they were there, could they? And even if they did, why would that stop them from attacking? Thomas and Beluil were only two and the pack probably contained as many as fifteen to twenty Fearhounds.

The sun had had dropped below the horizon, giving way to a quarter moon that provided little light and no warmth. A cold wind swept down from the north that presaged an early winter. Thomas and Beluil made camp where the Burren met the Highlands, putting a large, flat rock over the fire so as not to attract any attention. Beluil lay in a comfortable spot right in front of the fire, stretching out his long frame to soak in as much warmth as possible.

The Fearhounds had turned north and followed the Southern River out onto the Northern Steppes during the afternoon after darting in and out of the Highlands. Thomas and Beluil had gone as far as where the Southern River met the Sea of Mist before returning to the edge of the Burren.

The behavior of the pack bothered Thomas. Normally, Fearhounds wandered randomly during the hunt, searching for any prey that crossed their path. But not this time. Throughout the day the Fearhounds had traveled along the southern edge of the Highlands, and at regular intervals made at least a dozen quick forays into the Burren before returning to the Highland border. They had even entered Oakwood Forest.

They were hunting, but this time for something in particular. Maybe that's why they didn't come after him and Beluil. They were too busy with their search to bother. Thomas' curiosity got the better of him. He wanted to know what these Fearhounds pursued.

"We'll wait here, Beluil. When they come south again, we'll be ready."

47

AGGRAVATION

Kaylie left her father alone for the rest of the afternoon, deciding that she had pushed hard enough for the time being. As evening approached, Gregory led the troop along the bed of a small stream until it converged with another in the middle of a small glen. A hill sat at the juncture where the two streams formed into one.

As the soldiers set up camp for the night and started dinner, Kaylie wandered over to the hill. She thought it would be an easy climb to the top, but the tall grass that covered its sides deceived her. Several times she slipped as she tried to dig her feet into the hillside, and by the time she finally reached the top, beads of perspiration covered her forehead.

The hill topped the trees pushing in on the small glade her father had chosen as a campsite, allowing her to see for miles around. Below her the soldiers worked diligently at their tasks while Gregory surveyed everything with a practiced eye. That was interesting. From where she stood, Kaylie thought this hill, at some point in the past, might have actually been a waterfall. On both sides it appeared as if the forest ran up against the hill, which more and more looked like a cliff as she studied it. If her father decided to go in this direction tomorrow, they'd either have to climb up the hill or parallel the cliff until it tapered off again to level ground.

As she faced north, her breath caught in her throat. The snow-covered peaks of the Highlands towered over the trees, their huge forms speaking of strength and age. It was an awesome sight. She would do almost anything to have the opportunity to travel in the Highlands and see where Alessandra had assumed her place as leader of the most feared warriors in all the Kingdoms. Every day would be an adventure, filled with danger, excitement and fun.

"Kaylie, time for dinner," yelled her father, who stood at the base of the hill.

"Coming, father."

She took one last glimpse at the towering peaks. Someday, she promised herself. Someday.

48

STORIES

"Enough, Kaylie. You cannot train with Kael beyond the dagger. I will not change my mind so you might as well stop trying."

Dinner passed quietly after that as Gregory and Kaylie sat in front of a small fire, their backs up against a log dragged there by a few soldiers. Both were tired and hungry from the day's trek. The resemblance between father and daughter was remarkable, as both wore similar expressions of aggravation. When Kaylie finished her meal, she immediately started up again about learning how to use a sword. Tenacious almost to a fault, she refused to admit defeat. That same tenacity Gregory so admired most of the time was beginning to wear on his nerves.

"But—"

"No buts," said Gregory, cutting off his daughter. "I will not change my mind."

Kaylie slumped back against the log, crossing her arms and grimacing as if she had tasted something sour. He was impossible. Absolutely impossible! She had tried everything she could think of and still he refused to give in. It was like arguing with an oak tree.

"It would be so much easier if your mother were still with us," murmured Gregory, sighing as he poked at the fire with a stick. Sometimes he simply didn't know how to deal with his daughter.

Kaylie dropped the grimace from her face. "You miss her a lot, don't you?"

"Yes," he answered in a quiet, sad voice. "Yes, I do."

Kaylie looked at her father thoughtfully, weighing whether or not she should tell him what was on her mind. She decided that she might as well. He was already irritated with her so she didn't have much to lose.

"You shouldn't be alone, father. Mother has been gone a long time. I don't think she'd mind if you found someone else."

Gregory sat up, too surprised to know what to say. Thinking of nothing else, he replied in a huff, "I'm too old."

"You and I both know that's a lie," said Kaylie. "I know there are several women who are quite interested in getting to know you better. In fact, there's one who is more than just interested."

"Oh, really." Gregory leaned back against the log and crossed his arms, expecting his daughter to turn this conversation into a joke. "And just who might that be?"

"Sarelle Makarin."

"Sarelle," sputtered Gregory, sitting forward, his eyes wild for an instant.

"Yes, Sarelle Makarin. It is quite obvious by the way she looks at you that she's interested in much more than just the trade between our two kingdoms." Kaylie stretched her legs out, her self-satisfied grin spreading across her entire face. "Much more."

"But, she's—"

"Quite beautiful. Don't you agree? And very intelligent. She's also quite patient, which is an absolute necessity when it comes to you, father. You know, you can be quite difficult at times."

"Can I?" asked Gregory, his voice laced with sarcasm.

Kaylie failed to notice. "Yes, you can. And despite that she is quite taken with you."

"And just how do you know that?" The certainty in his daughter's voice frightened him. His worries from earlier in the day returned tenfold.

Kaylie smirked. "Oh, come now, father. Any woman could see it. Even you should by now. She sent you how many invitations to visit Benewyn? And when you finally said you couldn't, what did she do? She invited herself to Fal Carrach. Father, I'm quite disappointed in you. You really should have figured this out on your own."

"Yes, well, I had considered the possibility, but there were other things on my—"

"Actually, she's doing quite an excellent job of it."

"Job of what?" asked Gregory, his confusion obvious.

"Twisting you around her finger," chuckled Kaylie. "She's doing such a good job, you don't even know it."

"No woman can twist me around her finger," Gregory almost shouted in indignation. He looked around quickly, relieved that none of his men had heard him.

"Whatever you say, father," laughed Kaylie with delight, pleased that she could still tease him so easily. "Whatever you say."

She leaned over and gave him a kiss on the cheek. "Good night, father. I'm going to turn in." Kaylie rose from her place by the log and walked around the fire to where she had placed her blankets.

"Sarelle cannot twist me around her finger," Gregory protested a final time, but his daughter only laughed as she burrowed beneath her blankets.

Gregory got up as well, trying to get his mind thinking of

other things. He began to make a circuit of their small encampment. All the guards stood their stations as they should, he noted, pleased by their discipline. Yet, as he walked from one soldier to the next, he picked up on their uneasiness. Several fingered the hilts of their swords as if they expected a fight.

It wasn't long before Gregory felt it as well, the sense that there was something in the dark of the forest that shouldn't be there. It was a very uncomfortable feeling, especially when you didn't know the source. He shrugged it off. It was probably because they camped near the Burren. The stories of the dark and forbidding forest were legendary. But that's all they were. Stories. Nevertheless, before he turned in for the night he decided to double the guard. Just in case.

As he walked back toward the fire, his mind wandered back to the conversation he had just concluded with his daughter. Sarelle? Could Kaylie be right? She was extremely beautiful. And intelligent. And clever. But Sarelle? Why would she be interested in him? The whole thing confounded him. His hair had more grey than black, though he did have to admit that he was just as fit as he was when he was a youth. But Sarelle? He just couldn't believe it.

49

BLOODY SKIRMISH

Gregory woke with a start as shouts rang out in the small camp. The sun was still a distant wish. The perfect time for an attack, he thought, as he flung his blankets off and leapt to his feet, his sword already in his hand. He had considered taking off his boots before going to bed, but had decided against it because of the cold. He was glad that he did. He didn't have time to put them on.

Large black shadows that barely stood out against the early morning darkness flashed along the defensive perimeter established by his guards. Fearhounds — more than a dozen in all — and they were pushing his soldiers in toward the camp. He and his men had fallen into dire straits.

The beasts resembled large dogs, but that's where the resemblance ended. Many were the size of small ponies. Their jet-black fur made it extremely difficult to pick them out of the darkness. The only feature that remained visible for any extended period of time were their sharp, white teeth that rivaled many a dagger in size.

High-pitched howls tore through the night, setting the soldiers' teeth on edge. It was said the howl of a Fearhound sent bolts of terror through its prey, hence its name. Legend had it that these creatures, distant cousins to the wolves, followed the scent of fear. Once they had the scent, it was only a matter of time before they had the kill as well.

Gregory ignored the shivers of fear that ran up and down his spine and sprinted toward Kaylie. She had jumped up, her blankets tangled around her but her dagger in hand. At least she took Kael's words to heart. They had made camp at the base of the hill. None of the Fearhounds had come from that direction, so he pushed Kaylie behind him. His men had already formed a semicircle with their backs to the hill.

All his soldiers were veterans of dozens of border clashes, so there was no need for Gregory to give instructions. They knew the enemy they faced and what they had to do. Several more Fearhounds burst from between the trees to stand with the others, bringing the size of the pack to twenty. Counting his men, Gregory realized to his sorrow he had already lost five to the beasts. The odds definitely were not good. Still, he and his men would not go down without a fight.

He looked around the small glade, then up the hill, searching for a possible escape route for Kaylie. The only option he saw was going up the slope. But the Fearhounds would catch her easily even then. Cursing his luck, Gregory encouraged his men to hold strong. He knew in his heart, however, that it was a futile gesture.

Suddenly, the Fearhounds charged forward. His soldiers withstood the assault for several minutes, struggling valiantly to hold back the massive creatures. The men fought quietly, focused on their task and on their survival, their fear neatly locked away. Several nerve-shattering howls rose above the din of the swords striking out toward the beasts; the soldiers scored hits, yet to no avail. The skin of a Fearhound was almost as hard as rock, and though the beasts could be wounded, killing them was far from easy.

First one soldier was pulled down, and then another, and then another. Three bloody, red maws stared at Gregory as they feasted on their prey, their eyes promising that he would be next. It was a horrifying sight. His soldiers tried to close the breach in their defenses, but couldn't. The Fearhounds were too quick. Three beasts ran past the soldiers and sped directly for Gregory and Kaylie.

Gregory swung his sword in front of him in giant arcs, hoping the steel would keep the Fearhounds at bay. He saw the intelligence and cunning in their eyes now that they were so close. They would wait until he tired and then make their move. To speed up the process, the three Fearhounds split up. One remained in front of Gregory while the other two trotted to separate sides. Kaylie stayed behind her father, her dagger held at the ready as she spun from one side to the other on knees shaking with fear, trying to keep an eye on both Fearhounds.

The Fearhound in front of Gregory feinted forward. Just as Gregory moved to defend, the Fearhound on the left darted in as well. Gregory had expected that maneuver. Cursing their intelligence under his breath, he ignored the beast in front of him. Turning quickly, he swung viciously at the Fearhound moving in from his right. The Fearhound yelped more in surprise than pain as the steel bit into its flesh. However, what should have been a killing blow only resulted in a small slash across the beast's chest that momentarily halted its progress. The Fearhound growled in anger and charged straight at Gregory. At the same time the other two leapt forward.

Try as he might, he just wasn't fast enough. His blade again met the rush of the Fearhound, biting deeper into the creature's shoulder. The beast's rancid breath almost overpowered him. As the Fearhound staggered back, the one that had stood in front of Gregory leapt in the air, hoping to come down on his back. Catching the movement out of the corner of his eye, Gregory rolled away from the attack and jumped back to his feet. But the Fearhounds had succeeded. They had separated Gregory from Kaylie. Two of the creatures approached Gregory, while the third, limping slightly from the injury to its shoulder, stalked toward his daughter.

As the screams of his men, fighting and dying just twenty feet away, echoed in his ears, all he could think about was how to save his daughter from the death that awaited her. Before the two Fearhounds could attack him, Gregory charged forward, swinging his blade wildly. If he was going to die this day, he would do it on his own terms, fighting to his last breath trying to protect his daughter.

Kaylie tried to reach her father as he attacked the Fearhounds, but the injured beast remained where it was, sizing up its prey. She stood there in shock as the Fearhounds cut her off from her father, not knowing what to do. She had nowhere to go, nowhere to hide. She could barely stand as it was. Her knees continued to shake uncontrollably and her stomach did somersaults.

She thought of a dozen different ways to escape, but discarded them all, knowing in the end that it would be wasted effort. All she could do was go down fighting, just like the other soldiers. Yes, like the other soldiers. That thought made her feel a little better, and she slowly began to regain control of her legs. The queasy feeling in her stomach remained, however.

The Fearhounds weren't distracted for long. The injured beast walked stiffly toward her with bloodlust in its eyes, unafraid of her dagger. She took several steps back until her feet hit the base of the hill. Everything that Kael had taught her flashed through her mind in an instant. Though she tried to remember it all, it didn't really matter. Her dagger was of no use against a Fearhound. It wouldn't even be much of an annoyance.

Seeing her as an easy kill, the Fearhound continued to limp toward her confidently. Kaylie held the dagger in front of her, balancing on her toes just as she had been taught. She could hear her father yelling in anger as he tried to make his way past the two Fearhounds blocking his path, but she knew he would never get to her in time. She'd have to depend on her own abilities now.

When the Fearhound was no more than a few feet away, the creature lunged forward, its jaws aimed for her throat. Giving in to her instinct, Kaylie slashed with her dagger and then rolled to the ground, clear of the Fearhound's attack. The beast howled in pain. Kaylie had been true in her aim. Her slash dug into the slice caused by her father's sword. Though not a disabling blow, it was painful and would slow the Fearhound even more. If nothing else, at least she had scored a hit. Kael would have been proud of her.

The Fearhound lowered its head then, its eyes blazing red with anger. The beast leapt into the air, its sharp claws ready to tear into Kaylie. There was nothing she could do. She held the dagger in front of her, aimed for the Fearhound's chest. She knew she didn't stand a chance. If only she had learned how to fight with a sword! A dagger was such a pitiful weapon against a Fearhound. She could see the creature's sharp teeth and the saliva dripping off of them. She was going to die, and there wasn't a thing she could do about it.

Kaylie felt the Fearhound's hot breath on her face, the rank odor making her gag. Closing her eyes and gritting her teeth, she braced herself for the Fearhound's impact. Much to her surprise, she heard a loud thunk and then all was quiet around her. Hesitantly opening her eyes, she looked down. The Fearhound that just an instant before had seen her as an easy meal now lay at her feet, a long arrow sticking out of its eye. Its snout lay nearly on top of her bare toes, the Fearhound's spittle dripping down onto them. She jumped back, sickened by the sight of blood and saliva mixing on her flesh. She promised herself that she would never take her boots off outside of the Rock again.

More screams of pain rose above the din of battle. But this time they weren't coming from the soldiers. An arrow streaked down from the hilltop, and then another arrow right after the first, taking both the Fearhounds circling Gregory in the eye, killing them instantly. Gregory looked around in shock, searching for the source of unexpected aid.

More arrows fell from the sky, each one striking home with pinpoint precision. A Fearhound leaping through the air and about to tear out the throat of a wounded soldier tumbled in a heap to the ground. Another Fearhound turned away from its prey upon seeing one of its companions fall to the ground dead, only to meet its own death as an arrow tore through its brain.

Thomas calmly stood atop the hill, lost in the precision of his movements. Nock. Sight. Release. Nock. Sight. Release. Beluil stood before him, his teeth bared, ready to defend his friend if any Fearhound chose to attack. Thomas' mind was a complete blank. There was no thought. No feeling. Simply action. And as each arrow struck true, a small part of him rejoiced, imagining that every Fearhound destroyed was another prick in the skin of its master.

The remaining Fearhounds finally realized that they were under attack by a new foe and quickly located the source. Four of the creatures charged up the hill, howling their anger and snapping their jaws. Thomas waited there calmly, urging the creatures forward. He couldn't afford to miss now, so he waited just a second longer than necessary before releasing his first arrow. The second and third sped after it, and all three hit their targets, taking three of the Fearhounds in the eye and sending them tumbling back down the hill. The fourth was too close for Thomas to nock another arrow. Dropping his bow he reached for his sword, thinking he may have miscalculated. It proved unnecessary, however.

As the Fearhound lunged for Thomas, Beluil leapt as well. It looked like two shadows colliding in the early morning light. Smashing into the Fearhound in midair, Beluil clamped its powerful jaws on the beast's throat, tearing it out. The once fearsome creature fell to the ground lifeless. The entire skirmish came to an end in a matter of minutes.

"Thank you, my friend," whispered Thomas, bending down to pat Beluil affectionately on his head and make sure he was all right before picking up his bow.

Gregory and the soldiers who could still stand stared around them in amazement. Sixteen Fearhounds littered their small encampment, all with a long arrow sticking out of one eye, with three more at the base of the hill. None had ever seen such a feat before. The silence was deafening, as no one knew what to do. They didn't know how to handle the calm of a battle won that should have been lost.

Kaylie looked around as well, shivering as she measured with her eye the long white teeth of the Fearhound lying at her feet. She had come very close to dying, if not for the help of the unknown bowman. Shielding her eyes from the sun rising above the hill, her mouth opened in shock. The person on the hill did not appear as she had expected him to be.

She thought he would be tall and muscular and weathered. But he looked to be no more than a boy, and perhaps even her own age. A boy her own age? How could someone so young be so calm and confident, especially with four Fearhounds charging toward him? Who was he? How did he come to have a wolf — a very deadly wolf — as a pet? And why did he look so familiar? It all started to fit into place for her, the memories rushing back.

The boy looked down at them from his perch atop the hill, much like an eagle surveying its territory, and satisfied that everything was as it should be. For a brief moment, she thought their eyes locked, and she saw recognition in his. Much to her disappointment, his gaze passed over to her father, who stood there still as a statue just like his men.

Thomas examined the encampment, pleased to see that his and Beluil's efforts had not been wasted. Of the twenty soldiers, more than half remained standing. He briefly locked eyes with the girl, remembering their previous encounter, and again was captured by her beauty. He tore his eyes away with some reluctance, searching for the leader of the troop and finally settling on the large man just a few feet from the girl, his hair speckled with grey. Bringing the blade of his sword to his forehead, Thomas inclined his head to the man before walking across the hilltop and out of sight, Beluil trotting behind him.

The Highland bow. Gregory had not seen that since he last talked with Talyn Kestrel a few weeks before his murder. He couldn't believe what he had just witnessed. It had happened so fast, he could barely keep track of the fight. In less than two minutes, that boy — it had to be a boy, yet how that was possible he didn't know — had virtually wiped out a pack of Fearhounds all on his own, and had not even broken a sweat doing it. It was the most incredible thing he had ever seen. The same boy, he was sure, who had rescued his daughter in the Burren. Even now with the boy gone, he could make out the green eyes of their rescuer — the blazing green eyes hotter than any blacksmith's fire. Gregory sighed with relief, glad that he and his daughter still lived.

The spell of silence that had descended upon the soldiers during their rescue abruptly ended as the soldiers all started talking at once.

"Who was that boy?" asked one.

"Did you see that? Did you see that?" asked another.

"Probably one of the Sylvana," replied a grizzled soldier to the first question.

Another answered. "No, it couldn't be the Sylvana. There aren't any left."

"Maybe it's the Raptor," suggested a soldier who had been clawed on the leg but was still on his feet.

"No, that's just a story," replied the soldier who also had discounted the theory regarding the Sylvana.

"It must have been the Raptor," interrupted another, riding over his friend. "Because that was not a story that just saved us. Besides, who else can shoot so many of the beasts in the eye? It had to be the Raptor. That's the only explanation for it."

"Enough," shouted Gregory, cutting off the discussion. The soldiers looked at their leader as if they were boys whose hands had just been caught in the cookie jar. "See to the wounded. We're returning to the Rock. If we can be attacked once, we can be attacked again." The soldiers ran off to do as ordered.

Gregory walked over to Kaylie, taking her in his arms and hugging her. His heart had finally slowed to a normal rate.

"Father, you're hurting me," Kaylie said in a muffled voice, her face pressed up against her father's shirt.

He quickly released her. "Sorry," he said sheepishly.

"It's all right." Kaylie reached out and gave her father a hug as well.

"Are you hurt?"

"No, I'm fine," she replied. Her father's sigh of relief was audible.

"Good. I'm going to check on the wounded." As her father hurried off, he turned back to her. "By the way, you will start your sword training with Kael as soon as we get back."

Kaylie remained where she was, staring up the hill, her father's words washing over her and having no real effect. She had gotten what she wanted, and at the moment she didn't really care. An image of her rescuer's face appeared in her mind. In the Burren, just like now, and the wolf was with him then too. He had actually spoken to her then. She had never

thought that she would see him again, and like before now
hoped there would be a next time.

THE END

~

**Keep reading for the first three chapters of Book 4, *The
Makings of a Warrior*.**

BONUS MATERIAL

If you really enjoyed this story, I need you to do me a HUGE favor – please follow me on Amazon and BookBub.

And if you have a few minutes, consider writing a review.

Keep reading for the first three chapters of Book 4 of *The Sylvan Chronicles*, *The Makings of a Warrior*.

PETER WACHT

THE
MAKINGS
OF A
WARRIOR

4

THE
SYLVAN CHRONICLES

The Makings of a Warrior

By Peter Wacht

Book 4 of The Sylvan Chronicles

This book is a work of fiction. Names, characters, places, and incidents are the product of the author's imagination or are used fictitiously. Any resemblance to actual events, locales, or persons, living or dead, is coincidental.

Copyright 2019 © by Peter Wacht

Cover design by Ebooklaunch.com

All rights reserved. In accordance with the U.S. Copyright Act of 1976, the scanning, uploading, and electronic sharing of any part of this book without the permission of the publisher constitute unlawful piracy and theft of the author's intellectual property.

Published in the United States by Kestrel Media Group LLC.

ISBN: 978-1-950236-06-0

eBook ISBN: 978-1-950236-07-7

Library of Congress Control Number: 2019920372

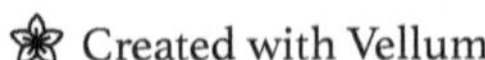 Created with Vellum

1. THE HUNGER

The hunger. It knew only the hunger. A desperate, unrelenting demand, one that could not be denied. As the years passed, the craving to complete its appointed task came and went, yet the hunger remained. To hunt. To kill. Then to hunt once more. It had never failed. It would not have survived for so long if it had. Created for a single purpose, if it failed, it died.

It had been a long time, though, since its last kill. Its hunger had increased as the days, then months, then years passed, becoming almost unbearable. But its prey still eluded it. Until now.

Flexing its arms and shoulders, leathery black wings opened and closed on its back. It had searched for a very long time, but to no avail. Now it could finally satisfy its hunger. Its prey, hidden for so many years, had finally shown itself. It was time to hunt. Time to kill.

2. THE PREY

"Thank you," said Thomas, patting the large black wolf on the back.

Without Beluil's assistance, Thomas very likely would have had his throat torn out by the last Fearhound. Only Beluil's quick action saved him.

Having tracked a pack of Fearhounds around the edge of the Burren, he and Beluil caught up to the beasts as they attacked a patrol from Fal Carrach, which also happened to include Fal Carrach's king, Gregory, and his daughter. Gaining the high ground above the skirmish, Thomas turned the tide with his precise shooting, every arrow striking true to take down a creature. Beluil eliminated the final Fearhound, which had gotten a bit too close for comfort.

Images flashed through Thomas' mind as he and Beluil walked deeper into the eastern part of Burren, slowly making their way back to the Isle of Mist. Harnessing his Talent, Thomas translated the images as "brothers." He understood. They had grown up together, he and Beluil. They were brothers. Other images followed.

"I am not in love," protested Thomas. Beluil relayed more

scenes of the girl Thomas had saved during the struggle with the Fearhounds. "I barely even looked at her."

Thomas' face turned beet red as he disavowed any interest in the raven-haired girl with penetrating blue eyes, much to Beluil's pleasure. The wolf's grin displayed all of his long, sharp teeth. Another image intruded on the others.

"Yes, well, we just won't tell her what happened, will we?"

Thomas eyed the wolf with suspicion. His grandmother Rya, barely five feet tall but with the presence of a queen, knew how to find out things that were supposed to remain secret. If she learned that Thomas and Beluil had taken on an entire pack of Fearhounds so soon after recovering from his injuries, her fury would know no bounds. He knew exactly what she would say, too: "Did we not raise you better, Thomas? You continue to take too many risks. One of these days, one of your decisions will come back to haunt you. And we will not be there to help you."

He understood that Rya just worried about him, and this was how she expressed it, but he really didn't want to sit through another lecture.

"What she doesn't know can't hurt her. Besides—"

A tickle along the back of his neck made him stop, his words forgotten. Beluil halted as well, recognizing the look on Thomas' face. The wolf scanned the forest around them, yet nothing seemed out of place. None of his acute senses warned him of danger. Thomas closed his eyes as the tickle increased in intensity, setting the hair on the back of his neck on end. His eyes would not help him now.

Something stalked them, something deadly. The subtle taint of evil drifted along the edge of his senses, much like a breeze bringing the scent of the sea when you were still a few miles from the coast. Sometimes you could taste the salty tang, sometimes you couldn't. The evil continued to flirt with his senses. It was getting closer, whatever it was, but he couldn't pinpoint its location.

Thomas took hold of the Talent, relishing the power of nature as it flowed within his blood. The trees and bushes around him suddenly buzzed with a new life that was hidden from those unable to harness the natural magic of the world. He extended his senses and searched the surrounding area again. Nothing. Thomas frowned. It had to be there. But where? He tried again, taking in more of the Talent. Yes, there it was. Off to his left. But he still could barely sense it, even though it inched toward him.

Thomas searched his memory as the feeling of evil teased him. Finally he had it. He recognized the source now. He and Beluil could try to escape — the thought of running passed through his mind, and it certainly was enticing — but it would do little good. The evil would continue the hunt until it found its prey; until it found him. The hunter was an assassin, the best the Kingdoms had ever known. At least now Thomas knew what he was up against and could use that to his advantage.

Beluil growled softly. Now he, too, sensed the approaching evil. Thomas reached for more of the Talent. There! He had the creature now. Off to his left for certain, no more than twenty feet away. Thomas relayed the information to Beluil, then opened his eyes and looked to the left with his peripheral vision. Still nothing. It was close to midday now, but the bright sun failed to penetrate the dense canopy of the Burren. The resulting shadows benefited their stalker.

Glad that he still held his sword, Thomas tried to calm his nerves as the evil moved steadily closer. It was a difficult thing to do. Since he couldn't see his enemy he'd have to wait until the creature made its move. That thought frightened him. All of his training urged him to attack. Standing still gave the assassin a potential edge. Now was the time. Strike! Strike now!

Thomas managed to rein in his emotions. Patience. Against this foe, it was the only thing that would allow him to survive.

The seconds passed slowly. Beads of cold sweat formed on his forehead. The evil continued its slow approach, unaware that Thomas tracked its movements. Eighteen feet. Fifteen feet. Thomas' mouth went dry. He resisted the urge to swallow. Soon. Very soon. He looked to his left again with his peripheral vision and this time picked out a shadow darker than the rest. A shadow that moved.

As the evil grew stronger, it felt as if a blacksmith were pounding out a horseshoe inside of Thomas' head. His mind cried out for action. To run or fight. Anything but just stand there. That was suicide. Fight, run, run, fight. Do something! Anything! Thomas ignored the pleas and watched the shadow as it glided toward him. Twelve feet. Ten feet.

Beluil could bear the wait no longer. Finally seeing their attacker clearly, he bared his teeth and leapt into the air, its claws extended. Much to the wolf's surprise, he failed to reach its target. Beluil was frozen in the air, unable to move a muscle. He couldn't even close his jaws to howl in anger. Dark Magic! Thomas made use of his friend's valiant effort, charging forward and swinging his blade with all his might.

Thomas' attack surprised the shadow, as it was not used to any response but fear. It quickly recovered, catching Thomas' sword on an armored forearm and turning it aside.

Just as Thomas had thought — a Nightstalker! That explained the futility of Beluil's attack. He had met one before when traveling with Rynlin. His grandfather had told him never to forget the feeling of evil from that experience, and he hadn't, much to his relief. Otherwise, he would already be dead. Using his Talent, Thomas created a ball of light that hung above his head, illuminating the forest and allowing him to see the assassin clearly.

The Nightstalker towered over Thomas, standing eight feet

tall with its skin the color of black granite. The ball of light hovering in the air prevented the creature from blending into the darkness as was its wont. Shaped like a man, its blood red eyes stared at Thomas. Its hunger was obvious. Thomas understood why his attack had not fazed the Nightstalker. Its body, covered in hard scales, served the same purpose as a soldier's armor.

Before Thomas could make use of the Talent once again, the Nightstalker attacked, swinging its scythe like claws at his face. Thomas parried the blows with his sword, their ferocity sending shivers down his arms. He unsuccessfully tried to break away from the attack. The Nightstalker followed after him, searching for a hole in Thomas' defenses.

Thankfully, the ball of light moved with them, preventing the assassin from slipping back into the shadows. Now out in the open, the Nightstalker pressed forward, its claws coming closer and closer each time to their intended target. If Thomas allowed this to continue, it wouldn't be long before his guts spilled out onto the forest floor.

Catching one of the Nightstalker's claws on his blade, Thomas ducked behind his attacker and ran back toward Beluil, who remained suspended in the air. Finally having some room to operate. Thomas gathered his will. A ball of fire shot from his palm, sizzling through the air toward the Nightstalker. The flames struck the Nightstalker full force, licking all over its body.

But just as quickly as they consumed the assassin, they died out. Thomas' momentary relief turned to worry. That's how Rynlin had killed the other Nightstalker. Why did it fail this time? Nightstalkers often had some skill in Dark Magic, which explained this one's ability to stop Beluil's attack, but he had never expected a Nightstalker to be so powerful.

Thomas had little time to ponder the possible reasons, as the Nightstalker again surged forward in search of blood. The evil grin on its face, exposing its sharp white teeth, almost unnerved Thomas. How was he supposed to defend himself against this creature if neither the sword nor the Talent worked? Thomas met the Nightstalker's attack and allowed the creature to force him backwards. He needed to find a solution. And fast.

As he retreated, parrying the teeth-jarring blows of the Nightstalker, an idea finally came to him. Mastering his will, Thomas drew on the Talent, allowing the power of nature to flow into his sword. He drew more and more of the power until the ancient steel blazed a deep blue.

This time, when the Nightstalker swung its claws toward Thomas' face, the creature danced back in pain. Its dark skin sizzled where it touched the blade. Sensing a shift in the momentum of the duel, Thomas lunged forward, swinging his blade high and low, each time forcing the Nightstalker to defend with an arm or wing. The hunter had become the prey.

The creature's skin burned horribly wherever Thomas' blade touched it. For the first time in its life, the Nightstalker entertained thoughts of escape. The blue flame of the blade blinded the creature, giving Thomas free rein to attack. As the assassin backed away, Thomas followed after relentlessly. Raising his blade above his head, Thomas swung it down with all his might. The Nightstalker moved to defend itself, raising its claws to meet the attack.

The deception worked. In mid-motion, Thomas changed the direction of the blade and brought it in from the side, catching the creature below the shoulder. The pulsating blue blade easily sliced into its skin, digging halfway into its body. The Nightstalker's scream of pain sent chills through Thomas. Tearing the blade out of the creature's body, he jumped back. The Nightstalker fell to its knees, the horrible wound pouring dark red blood onto the forest floor. The look of surprise on the creature's face disintegrated as it collapsed in the grass.

Thomas lowered his blade, a wave of exhaustion rolling over him. He released the Talent and the blue blade winked out, becoming steel once more. Relief spread through him. For the first time in his life he realized just how close he had come to dying. Thomas felt a warm nose on his hand. Beluil stood by his side once more. With the Nightstalker's death, the wolf had gained his freedom from the spell.

"It looks like we're even," said Thomas, patting the wolf affectionately on the head.

3. A VISIT

Killeran sat gloomily in his travel tent, his feet propped up on a footrest. It was all that remained of his fort. Once a symbol of his power in the Highlands, it was now nothing more than a burned out wreck. More than half of his men were dead or deserted, and his center of power, his primary tool for holding sway in the foothills of the Highlands, was destroyed. Even the massive steel cages that once held his Highland slaves were now simply twisted masses of steel.

He took another gulp from his wine bottle, hoping it would help him think. He had to do something quickly. But what? He barely had enough men to protect himself now, even with his warlocks. Some of his surviving reivers who had gone after the escaped Highlanders spoke of the use of Dark Magic. He drained down a quarter of the wine in his bottle. That was absolutely preposterous! No Highlander had displayed such a skill for hundreds of years, much less would have any control over Dark Magic.

Killeran turned his thoughts back to his current dilemma. He had determined that his men had latched on to an excuse, needing some way to explain their incompetence. Killeran didn't care for excuses. He smiled as he remembered the shock on their faces when he ordered them drawn and quartered. He didn't want excuses; he wanted results.

Even worse, he now had no supplies. How was he supposed to rebuild his fort and begin mining again without any wood, or steel, or even more important, workers? Since the destruction of the Black Hole the Highlanders had gone to ground, and he didn't have the ability to pursue them in the higher passes now. As a result, his reivers now had to do the mining themselves. Though they weren't happy about it, the error of their ways had quickly been shown to them by some of the warlocks. However, these two concerns were inconsequential compared to the third. Somehow Rodric had learned of the escape.

Taking another drink from the bottle, he glanced off to the right where he had thrown the crumpled missive from the High King. *I will not tolerate such incompetence*, the bastard had written. *Only a fool would allow two boys to cause such problems. If you cannot handle your affairs properly, then perhaps a new Regent of the Highlands would be in order. And as you know, much like a king or queen, there is only one way to remove a regent from his throne.*

Killeran cursed himself for the thousandth time in the past six weeks. He knew he should have killed those two. He knew it! But he had ignored the warnings that had gone off in his head. And because of it, he huddled in a stinking tent, drinking wine that had almost turned to vinegar and digging out precious little gold and minerals for a High King he despised.

Killeran threw the bottle of wine to the ground in disgust, watching it shatter into a thousand pieces. He wanted to lash out, but at what? He had already punished the few remaining men who had failed to recapture the Highlanders, but the pleasure from that experience had not lasted long enough.

Slouching back in his chair, he ran a hand under his dripping nose. This damn Kingdom! It seemed that this cold had plagued him ever since he entered this cursed wilderness. He had to think. He had to find someone to blame. Otherwise, he would have more to worry about than just a snot-nosed, whiny High King. He'd have to worry about someone who could snuff out his life in—

"Another Nightstalker is dead."

Killeran jumped up from his chair, spinning around. The voice sounded like a hiss, similar to wind escaping through a barely open window. It set Killeran's teeth on edge, yet he could not locate the source. It couldn't be. How could he know so soon? How could he be here?

"I know everything, Killeran. I am everywhere."

Killeran spun around again, looking into the shadows of the tent but finding nothing. His heart raced with terror. How could—

"I am here, Killeran, though you may not see me." The voice was quiet, dangerous, sure of its power. "You do not show me the proper respect."

Killeran immediately dropped to his knees and bowed his head to the ground. "Master, I am sorry." His body shook with terror, and he could do nothing to stop it.

"That's better, Killeran. I'm glad to see that you still retain some of your manners." The raspy voice, though soft, filled the tent with its presence. The power behind the voice terrified him.

"The warlocks failed me, Master," began Killeran, his mind churning at a furious pace in search of an excuse. "If not for them—"

"Save your breath, Killeran. You think to lie to me? To me? I am the Master of Lies, Killeran! Yet you try to trick the Oath-breaker?"

The dry whisper became a shout that shook the tent poles. The structure swayed violently, threatening to collapse.

Killeran sank into the carpet as far as he could, desperate to escape the voice, yet knowing in his heart that he could not. He would never be able to escape. He mumbled something incoherent, his fear usurping his reason.

"You will listen to me, Killeran, and do exactly as I say. Is that understood?"

Killeran nodded his head vigorously, eager to please. Even more eager to stay alive.

"Good. As I said, the Nightstalker is dead. He pursued a green-eyed boy. I'm sure you are familiar with him."

Green-eyed boy? The Kestrel whelp! He had been a fool. A complete fool. Everything came flooding back to him. Months before Chertney had told him to look for a green-eyed boy, but he had not paid much attention. He didn't pay much attention to anything Chertney said. And now look where it had gotten him. But why send a Nightstalker after a boy? And how could the Nightstalker have died? Was that even possible?

"Yes, it's possible," answered the raspy voice, reading Killeran's mind. "I'm glad to see that you admit your incompetence, if only to yourself. I have a new task for you, Killeran. You will succeed this time. If you don't, it will be your last."

Killeran nodded, almost banging his head on the ground. Relief swept through him. Just seconds before he was certain he was about to die. But he had been given a respite, for now. He would make good use of it.

"You will find this boy — this Highlander — and you will eliminate him. Do you understand?"

Killeran nodded.

"He has escaped me for too long."

"Yes, Master. He will be found."

"Good," said the voice. "And to speed you in your task, remember this, Killeran. You have failed me once. Don't fail me again. Otherwise this boy's death will be pleasant compared to your own." Just as quickly as the voice came, it ended.

Killeran remained on his knees, bending his head in submission for several minutes more. He told himself it was a sign of respect for his Master, and not the result of his paralyzing fear. He was still alive. Killeran sighed with relief and fell forward into the carpet. He would need several more bottles of wine this evening. Several more.

I hope you enjoyed the first three chapters. To keep reading *The Makings of a Warrior*, Book 4 of *The Sylvan Chronicles*, you can order your copy from my author website or Amazon.

www.PeterWachtBooks.com

This short story is a prelude to the events in my series *The Tales of Caledonia* and is free to readers who receive my newsletter.

Join Peter's newsletter and get your FREE short story at www.PeterWachtBooks.com.

www.ingramcontent.com/pod-product-compliance
Lightning Source LLC
Chambersburg PA
CBHW051508030726

47592CB00006B/2160